PROPOSING CHRISTMAS

A VICTORIAN CHRISTMAS ROMANCE

ELLIE ST. CLAIR

Facebook: Ellie St. Clair

Cover by AJF Designs

Do you love historical romance? Receive access to a free ebook, as well as exclusive content such as giveaways, contests, freebies and advance notice of pre-orders through my mailing list!

Sign up here!

Also By Ellie St. Clair

Christmas Books

Proposing Christmas
A Match Made at Christmas
A Match Made in Winter
Christmastide with His Countess
Her Christmas Wish
Merry Misrule
Duke of Christmas
Duncan's Christmas

For a full list of all of Ellie's books, please see
www.elliestclair.com/books.

CHAPTER 1

"*W*e've lost everything."

Lady Noelle Sinclair could only blink and stare in disbelief at her father's confession.

Finally, she closed her eyes, cleared her throat, and calmly folded her hands in her lap. "Please explain." She was proud that her tone was much more even than the turmoil inside her. She had suspected they were struggling, but this was more than she had imagined.

"Well," her father said, shifting his narrow figure back and forth from one side of the faded damask chair to the other, the rosewood at the backing creaking. Noelle wasn't sure if he was searching for physical comfort or emotional. "You know I made a few investments recently," he began.

"I do," Noelle said from between tight lips. "Investments that I advised you against. How often have I told you that if something sounds too good to be true, it probably is?"

"Ah, love, you are wise beyond your years."

1

"Please do not placate me," Noelle said, taking a deep breath and letting it out slowly. Her father was a good man, truly he was, but he was also one of the most gullible people she had ever met. As soon as someone told him a story that played to his emotions, he would part with any pound he could find.

It seemed that he had finally reached the bottom of his pocket.

"Very well," her father said with a sigh, placing his chin on his hands. "My stock in this company was supposed to be worth a fortune. The company was to develop a new railway once all shareholders paid in – and many people purchased shares, mind you. A railway greatly needed, leading to Cornwall."

"Father, you knew that several of these companies are speculative or fraudulent."

"Yes, but many of my friends were involved in this one, as was a key investor who always gets these things right. The man at the helm had proven himself in the past with other developments. Why would this one be any different?"

"So, what happened?"

"Once the money was deposited, he disappeared," her father sighed, running his hand over the few hairs remaining on his nearly bald head. "He better not show his face here again." He leaned in toward her. "I know you think I misjudged this, Noelle, but even Cooper Hartwell invested."

"Cooper Hartwell?" she raised her eyebrows. She had never met the man, but he was known to be one of London's shrewdest and wealthiest businessmen. Cutthroat and willing to do anything necessary to get ahead. Most of her father's friends spoke of him with derision, but Noelle had always guessed they feared what a man like him represented – a threat to their social status, for he came from nothing, his wealth was newly earned. "What does he have to say about it?"

"I haven't spoken to the man," her father said, rubbing his chin. "Perhaps I should."

"Is there any way to recover your losses?" Noelle asked as she rose from her chair, unable to sit still any longer. She crossed her arms over her chest and walked to the window of the drawing room, looking down over the empty street below. Even the trees seemed sad, having lost most of their leaves by now as the weather had cooled.

"No," her father said, his tone so glum that Noelle had to turn around to assess him. "Everything's gone. When I say everything, Noelle, I mean everything. I am over my head in debt, with only my title keeping me out of debtor's prison. I've sold everything we have to sell. All I have left is this London house – for now. This investment was my last hope."

"And you have no son to marry off for a large dowry," Noelle murmured. Meanwhile, she was nothing but a burden.

"I'm afraid that I will struggle to find an advantageous match for you, Noelle," her father said with a sigh, hanging his head. "Your mother would be so disappointed in me."

"I was supposed to ensure that nothing like this happened to you," Noelle said, walking over and placing a hand on her father's shoulder. "I failed in that. Do not fret about such a marriage for me. I would prefer to choose my husband. If I cannot find one, so be it. I am more than capable of providing for myself."

Her father placed his head in his hands then and did something that shocked Noelle more than his entire confession – he sobbed.

She could only place an arm around him and try to comfort him, even as it felt like the house was crumbling around her, brick by brick. Her father meant well and had always done what he thought was best for her, but her mother had been the wise one in the marriage. Since her death, Noelle had vowed to take care of this little family of theirs. If only she had the opportunity to look after all the financial endeavors.

"Before we lose all hope, Father, we need to see if we can fight for what we lost."

"How?" he choked out as she gripped his shoulders.

"You said Cooper Hartwell was involved?"

He nodded. "Yes. But I do not see why he would take an audience with me."

"You may be ruined, but you are still a viscount, and that has to mean something, even to a man like him," she said, moving her fingers together in thought. "We will have to try to encounter him by accident and then see if we can discuss this with him."

The slightest hint of a plan providing her a modicum of hope, she nodded and patted her father's shoulder again.

"I'll figure this out," she said. "Just leave it to me."

* * *

COOPER HARTWELL DRUMMED his fingertips on the desk before him, silently seething.

No one got the better of him.

No one.

Fortunately, he had been more reserved than usual in his investment with Albert Sanderson's railway company, but a loss was a loss.

However, he had to set that aside momentarily, for he had a far greater opportunity sitting in front of him.

But one that was just out of his reach.

Cooper was on the cusp of taking a great leap forward to

achieve all he had set out to accomplish, but one thing was holding him back.

His birth.

Or, that is, the utter lack of status he had been born into. On the foundation of pure grit, hard work, and wise investments, he had grown a company that had everything in place to build his own railroad – to hell with putting his faith or his wealth with anyone else.

But no one would completely trust a man without any social connections besides those he had bought.

"Why are you so ornery this afternoon?" his brother asked, standing in the doorway and studying him.

Cooper reminded himself to store his brandy exports somewhere his brother could not find them. It had taken Cooper far longer than it should have to realize that Trenton only cared for his imports because he felt they were his own personal supply.

"I am not ornery," Cooper snapped back before stopping and chuckling at himself. "Fine. Perhaps I am ornery today. But I have good reason for it."

"Because that bastard Sanderson stole your money?"

"I should say I have *multiple* good reasons. One is Sanderson. I thought the railroad a sound idea and was known to never miss. Now, I've likely ruined much of my chances with these gentlemen. They won't trust me again."

"You don't have the answers to everything," Trenton said before hiccupping loudly. "You just think you do."

Cooper rolled his eyes as he stood and began pacing. "I need an in."

"An in where?"

"To a seat at the table."

At Trenton's confused look, Cooper shook his head and tried again with patience for his brother. Cooper might have spent years studying to become the man he was today, but

Trenton had been occupied with other, less savory, activities. "Not an actual table. Some men receive better contracts because they are at events and in clubs with the men who invest, sell land, compose government, and make these decisions. To them, I am a threat to all they know."

Trenton pulled a hunk of bread out of his pocket and bit into it, causing crumbs to drop onto the floor. Cooper didn't want to know when and where it had come from.

"How'd they get there?" he asked lazily, but Cooper's head turned sharply toward his brother as the question was decent.

"They are part of the noble set themselves."

"Born into it?" Trenton said before strolling into the room and throwing himself into one of the chairs. "Never stopped you before."

"No," Cooper said, tapping his chin with his index finger. "It hasn't. And now that you say that – *most* of them were born into it. But not all."

"So…"

"Some married into it."

"Married?" Trenton launched out of the chair, one boot flying off his foot as he did. "You're taking a wife?"

Cooper shook his head, not affected by Trenton's outburst, for his brother was always easily shocked.

"No, I have no interest in marrying," he said as Trenton sat again. Marriage would tie him down, and Cooper's ambitions were far too high to have to worry about a wife at home. A housekeeper could look after his house, and other women could satisfy his more carnal needs. A wife might expect emotion, love, even. Cooper didn't have that in him.

"But perhaps if I found the right connection – for a time – I can still achieve my aim." He pushed away from his chair and began to pace around the room, rubbing his chin as he thought of it. "What I need, Trenton, is an invitation to a few elite social events. Once I am there, it should be easy to find my way back. I've been able to work my way into any group of people, have I not?"

"I suppose," Trenton grumbled. "The ladies do seem to enjoy your company."

"They do," Cooper said with a grin. "All I need to do is charm a few hostesses, and there I will be, at every social event or gathering where I can talk to their husbands. Eventually, I will be wealthy enough that my riches will speak for me when a title does not. All I need is some credibility to start."

"How will you go about building that?" Trenton asked. "You cannot walk up to a lady and demand that she introduce you to her peers."

"Of course not," he said. "You're right about that. I need to attend an event where I might meet someone. Where I can casually entertain the idea of searching for a wife, as there won't be any other way to attract interest in a young lady of noble birth. A charity event, perhaps. They always allow us entrance when they need our sizeable donations."

"So, you'll pretend you are interested in marriage and then be done with this woman once you achieve your aim?" Trenton asked, now swinging one leg back and forth over the arm of his chair.

"You don't need to put it quite like that."

"But that's the way of it."

"I suppose. But I will not be so callous about it."

"Doubt she'll see it that way."

"Did I ask for your help?" Cooper said, his patience with his brother once again failing.

"No," Trenton said with a grin, finding joy in Cooper's annoyance with him. "But you need it, whether you like it or not. You never would have come up with this diabolical idea without me."

"Stop making me out to be such an ass."

"I only speak the truth," Trenton said with a shrug as he drunkenly pushed himself to his feet and walked out of the room. "You can always count on me for that."

Cooper sighed and pushed his hands into his pockets as he watched him go.

His brother wasn't wrong about that.

Cooper just hoped he wasn't right about the rest of it as well.

CHAPTER 2

$\mathcal{N}$oelle stood at the side of the main ballroom at Willis' Rooms, surveying the crowd before her. She had asked around as surreptitiously as she could about Cooper Hartwell's suspected activities. She had heard from their sole remaining maid who had heard from another maid who had heard from her lady that the lady's mother, Lady Burton, had invited him to her charity event held for the orphans at the hospital in St. Giles.

Noelle was well aware that this event was constructed only to give Lady Burton something to do and help others believe she was a most benevolent benefactor.

But if it helped others in the process, then so be it.

Noelle, of course, would be unable to add anything of significance to the purse for the orphans, but her presence here would have to suffice.

Her perusal of the room had to pause for a moment, however, when she was joined by one of her closest friends, Hattie George, daughter of Lady Burton herself.

"Hattie, how lovely to see you!" Noelle said with a large smile for her friend.

"I am so glad you came," Hattie said, taking her hand. "I was worried there would be no one in this room worth speaking to."

"I always find events such as these of great interest," Noelle said, "for it is not just the usual invitees that we typically find in attendance."

"Do you notice how divided the room is?" Hattie whispered. "It is as though we asked the *ton* to stand on one side and the newly rich on the other. Although, there is a great deal of interest from one side in the other."

"The unfamiliar holds great intrigue, is that not so?" Noelle said with a raised eyebrow.

"This is true," Hattie agreed. "Anyway, this is the last event that we will attend, let alone host, before we leave for the country. Will you be staying in London?"

"No, I do not suppose I will be," Noelle said, bitterness touching her lips. For they would not be leaving simply because the Season was over. Instead, it was because they would have to sell their London home and retreat to the one property left – the entailed estate, which they couldn't sell even if they wanted to.

Which they didn't, for that would be saying farewell to all they had ever held dear.

"If you and your father are alone for Christmas, you know you are always welcome to come stay with us," Hattie said cheerfully. Noelle appreciated this, for Hattie was the one person she had trusted with a few of her secrets, including the fact that they were in debt—although she hadn't told her just how much so.

"Thank you, Hattie, that is kind," Noelle said, although her attention suddenly wavered.

She had been looking for Cooper Hartwell since she had arrived, based on the description she had been provided. Noelle had assumed that when she was finished with this conversation, she would have to seek him out, but it didn't seem that was going to be necessary.

She knew the moment he entered the room. The crowd seemed to part as he walked through them, his enigmatic authority causing a stir. That wasn't the only reason he captured her attention, however. The moment Noelle caught sight of him, her stomach twisted into a ball of knots, for she had to prevent herself from walking toward him.

It was the first time Noelle had seen him, yet she knew it was him before Hattie even said anything.

He was tall, his shoulders broad, his dark hair swirling over his forehead in a swoop. As he passed, his eyes flicked over them, and Noelle had to force herself to swallow when she saw the glint in those navy blue eyes that passed over her.

"Cooper Hartwell," Hattie confirmed. "Mother will be absolutely thrilled he attended. He is always known for his generous donations."

"Do you know him well?" Noelle asked once she found her voice, and her friend shook her head.

"No. Mother has suggested inviting him to a few house parties, but Father will not hear of it – at least not yet. I do believe that he is weakening. Soon, we will be unable to ignore the fact that there are men such as he who have wealth far greater than those such as my father and yours have ever had."

Or their ancestors ever did.

"Do you believe it?" Noelle asked. "That such men could threaten our way of life?"

"It is not as though they are going to inherit a title or enter the House of Lords," Hattie said with a shrug. "So no, I do not believe so."

Before Noelle could continue, Hattie sighed, and Noelle followed her gaze across the room to where Lady Burton was waving her hand toward Hattie, the feathers on her hat bobbing emphatically with the effort.

"My mother is calling for me, likely to have me try to charm some young man into parting with some of his riches. I do not know why she continues to believe I can do so. She is far too used to my sister. Hermione is much better at such flirtations than I could ever be. She must have already been put to work."

"Be yourself, Hattie, and they will be charmed," Noelle said with a parting smile to her friend before she slipped into the crowd, trying to make herself invisible. Lady Burton had hired artists for the event who sat in the middle of the room, painting anyone brave enough to pose as a subject. It was actually rather intriguing.

She caught sight of Mr. Hartwell and stopped near him, pretending to watch one of the painters at work as she eavesdropped on his conversation.

"Trenton," he was saying in a low voice that Noelle could only just make out. "Not helpful."

"You said you were trying to find a wife!" the other man exclaimed, his accent rough and his tone pleading. "This girl seemed desperate."

"*She* was desperate for a man. Her father is half as wealthy as I am. They don't need me. The *family* has to be desperate for my wealth to agree to me. The woman can't be invested in this relationship. I'm not a monster."

Well, this was interesting. Why would a man like Cooper Hartwell seek a bride – and a bride who required his riches?

"How long 'til you'll be rid of the girl?"

My goodness, was he planning a murder?

"Until after Christmas. By then, I should be able to make my connections and let her go quietly. We'd agree on a reasonable explanation to prevent scandal."

He lowered his head, his voice too quiet for Noelle to

hear the rest of the conversation, but she had heard enough. Perhaps Cooper Hartwell might have more to offer her than simply assistance retrieving their lost investment. A family desperate for wealth? She was part of one. A woman who would not be too invested in the relationship? She was the girl. She only had to ensure that her family didn't walk away without compensation.

"Mr. Hartwell, is it?" she said, boldly stepping beside him.

He tilted his head toward her, taking his time perusing her from her head to toes and back again before his lips curled in greeting, although not quite a smile.

"I do not believe I have had the pleasure of making your acquaintance," he said, his voice more cultured than it had been before when speaking to his brother, low and rumbling, stirring some previously dormant desire deep in her core.

"I am Lady Noelle Sinclair," she said. "I believe you know my father, Lord Walters."

"I have heard of him," he said, his navy blue eyes glinting immediately in recognition. Noelle wasn't sure if that was a good sign or a bad one, but she would have to accept it.

"I understand this is rather untoward, but would you come to speak with me somewhere more private?"

"Will your father be accompanying us?"

"No. But he will approve of what I must speak to you about. I can promise you that."

"As much as doing so is likely a rather poor decision on my part, you have me intrigued, Lady Noelle," he said in that deep voice that caused her very soul to vibrate. "And that is a feat, indeed."

* * *

COOPER FOLLOWED the mysterious young woman through the ballroom, out the doors, and into a small alcove overlooking the gathered crowd below. It would be the perfect place for a tryst, not that he was out to ruin anyone. He was here to entice a young lady, not entrap one.

However, if there was ever a temptress, she was walking in front of him, the picture of grace and elegance. Her presence effortlessly commanded attention, as she had approached him with confidence yet without a hint of arrogance.

Her auburn hair was pulled back away from her face into a low chignon at her neck in the polished style of the day. Unruly tendrils escaped it, however, as though she had a spirit within her that was trying to break free.

As much as he enjoyed watching her walk before him, he longed to see her face again. He recalled the luminous skin that glowed naturally over high cheekbones, a delicate nose, and a well-defined jawline, with deep, expressive, warm brown eyes gazing up at him. Full and naturally tinted, her lips curved into a smile that lit up her face, even if he could tell she had ulterior motives in mind. What those were remained to be seen.

When she finally found a place in the shadows that she deemed appropriate, she stopped and turned to him as she sat.

He had no choice but to obey, even though it put them in decidedly close proximity.

"So, tell me, *Lady* Noelle," he drawled, wanting to set her in as much unease as he felt, "what can I do for you?"

"I have a problem," she said promptly.

"Doesn't everyone?"

"They do. That is exactly the point."

"Continue."

He couldn't decide whether he wanted her to get straight to it or draw this out to give him additional opportunity to listen to her speak. Which wasn't like him at all. Usually, he didn't stand for bullshit.

"You have a problem as well," she continued, and he couldn't help but smirk back at her.

"Do I, now?"

"You do. I overheard you speaking to your brother."

"You were listening to me?" he made a tsking sound, chastising her outwardly, even though he was cursing his brother and himself inwardly. He should have known better. Someone always overheard things at such events. He should have left Trenton at home.

"I was standing near you and couldn't help but hear," she said with a shrug. "It wasn't purposefully. That is why some conversations are best to be had in private. As we are doing now."

He could only nod, his jaw tight. She was right, even if he didn't like it.

"I am guessing that you have brought me here because you have a solution to both of our problems?"

"Ah, Mr. Hartwell, luck alone did not create your success."

"Most assuredly not."

"Well, then, my bright investor, here is the situation." She took a breath, and for the first time, Cooper saw the vulnerability hovering in her eyes, and he realized that it would cost her to share this piece of information with him. "You were involved in an investment recently that turned out to be nothing more than a scam."

"Sanderson's railroad," he said curtly, annoyed all over again.

"Yes." She nodded. "My father was part of that as well. Do you see any scenario where we will ever see this money again?"

"No," he said, pursing his lips. "We were all fools for providing any bit of our wealth. Albert Sanderson is gone and our money with him. It's not worth the effort to chase him down."

"I was afraid you would say that, although I had hoped that a man like you might better understand how we might recover it. It might not be worth your effort, but it could mean everything to my father."

"If your reason for bringing me here is to try to convince me to help you, then I am afraid that I will have to disappoint you," he said, finding that she wasn't the only one who might be disappointed. He had been hoping she had a more intriguing offer.

The truth was, he was becoming bored with his usual business plans, and he had rather hoped that Lady Noelle might have something of interest for him. But it was just the usual – someone searching for a bleeding heart that he most assuredly did not possess.

"That is not all," she said, placing a hand over his when he stood to walk away, holding him there. He tried to ignore the tingle where her hand had touched his.

"No?"

Was that his heart rate increasing in pace? Usually, only the thrill of a new business deal caused it to pick up.

"I have a proposal for you, Mr. Hartwell," she said, meeting his eyes.

He should walk away. What could this girl possibly have to offer him that he could be enticed to accept? Yet he couldn't seem to tear himself away.

"Yes?"

"Marry me."

CHAPTER 3

They both stayed rigid for a moment, stopped in a tableau that one of the artists below would likely long to paint, until Mr. Hartwell finally moved from his crouched position to a full stand.

"I am afraid that you have the wrong idea," he said, his face hardening as he stepped backward. Was that fear in his expression? "I am not interested in a wife."

"Forgive me. I was unclear," Noelle said, mortification overwhelming her momentarily. She had been so caught up in Mr. Hartwell's presence. His navy eyes drew her in, the quick expressions he tried to hide keeping her there.

She could understand now why he was so successful. It was not just his handsome features but the mysterious allure about him.

"I am not suggesting that we *actually* marry." She breathed deeply, attempting to center herself and return to her mission. "I am suggesting that we fake an engagement. From what I heard, you need the opportunity to integrate yourself with the nobility. I can provide that opportunity for you. My father – for now – is well respected, and before she died, my mother was a well-known hostess with many friends in the *ton*. I am happy to make you whatever connections you require."

He coolly assessed her. "And in exchange?"

This was the tricky part. She inhaled courage.

"In exchange, I would ask that you pay off my father's debts."

"What kind of debts are we talking about?"

"Over fifty thousand pounds," she said, hurrying forward as his eyes widened. "I would not expect you to pay all of it but a portion. Before we enter into a contract, we can ascertain the exact number."

"A contract?" The corner of his lips tipped upward. "It seems you are a businesswoman yourself, Lady Noelle."

A flush stole up her cheeks, but she would not allow this man to intimidate her, even if he was not doing so purposefully.

"I would want this to be fair to both of us," she said. "My father has lost a great deal on bad investments. I am not asking that you rescue us completely, but only that you cover enough so that we do not lose all respectability."

"Respectability is so important," he said sarcastically, annoying her, and she raised an eyebrow toward him.

"Is that not what you are currently chasing?"

He stared at her in surprise for a moment before he threw back his head and laughed.

She could only blink in astonishment until he finally settled once more.

"You are quick-witted, Lady Noelle. I like that. How long would you propose this last?"

"I would suggest that I pose as your fiancée for the holiday season. My friend Lady Hattie – her mother is Lady Burton, who is hosting this event today – is having a party over Christmastide and she has invited me and my father.

You could attend as well, as my betrothed. Many influential guests stay over the season, and this year, we can even take the railway there as it has just been extended to meet the town. After Christmas, we could amiably part ways."

He crossed his arms, and she wished she could read his thoughts, for his face gave nothing away.

"You have an interesting proposition."

"And?"

"I am intrigued but hesitant. If you know society as well as you claim, would you truly be willing to deceive them? Your friends? Your family? If – and I mean *if* – we go ahead with this, I would want no one to know the terms of our arrangement, during or after. Gentlemen would hardly be inclined to follow my ideas if they knew I used a young lady this way."

"I am the one suggesting it."

"Yes, but no one would believe it," he scoffed. "I also would prefer not to break your heart. What if you fell in love with me?"

It was her turn to laugh now. "You have a high opinion of yourself, Mr. Hartwell," she said. "I can assure you that my head has not been overwhelmed with thoughts of a man before, and it certainly isn't going to start now. Besides," she leaned in, "maybe *you* will fall in love with *me*. What if, Mr. Hartwell, after all of the success you find in business, you will lose something so valuable to a woman?"

He grinned wickedly. "I enjoy women, Lady Noelle, but I can assure you that my heart is not available to anyone. Most especially not a noblewoman."

"Very well, then," she said, trying not to be insulted and holding up a finger before he could continue. "I must tell you that I would have another stipulation."

"It sounds like this will be one of the more complex contracts I have signed."

"There will be no romantic gestures unless we are in public. I know people will need to see affection between us to believe in an engagement, but I will not be ruined."

"Of course," he said so easily that she wondered if he had any attraction toward her at all. Not that it mattered. "Can you honestly say that you have no hesitations?"

She paused. Of course she did, but she wasn't inclined to share them with him. "There is always uncertainty in aligning oneself with a person one doesn't know."

"Some would say that aligning with a friend could be even worse for the fallout has greater consequences."

"Perhaps," she said, tilting her head. "But at this point, the alternative is complete ruin. I could face the surety of losing one of our homes, our staff, most of my possessions, and, quite possibly, my father. On the other hand, I could go forward with the possibility that you could restore our fortunes enough that my father could make a go of it again."

"This last investment was the only one I have ever entered that has failed miserably," he said.

"I see."

"I told myself I would not make a bad investment again." He leaned in toward her, seizing the space in front of her. "Tell me, Lady Noelle, can you assure me that investing in you will benefit me?"

"I can assure you that I always uphold my end of a deal, Mr. Hartwell," she said, finding her throat so thick she could hardly breathe, let alone speak. "You have nothing to fear."

"Very well, then," he said, narrowing his eyes and breathing in slowly and deeply. "Consider us engaged."

A strange combination of relief and fear rushed over Noelle. Relief that she had found a way forward, out from this hole her father had dug for them. And fear of what this arrangement would mean. Close quarters with Mr. Hartwell, at the very least. But she could handle it. He was just a man, albeit a tall, handsome, intelligent, intimidating one.

She held out her hand. "It will be a pleasure doing business with you, Mr. Hartwell."

He looked down at her hand but did not attempt to take it.

"Pleasure it will be, I'm sure," he agreed. "I do not believe this type of agreement should be sealed with a handshake, however."

"No?" she said, dropping her hand and feeling foolish. She was a woman. Of course, he wouldn't see this as a business deal.

"*This* should be sealed with a kiss," he said, leaning in and capturing her lips.

* * *

COOPER COULDN'T HAVE SAID what had come over him.

He had been seeking a business arrangement in which the woman would have no feelings toward him and would be solely interested in his money.

But then, this temptress had offered him precisely what he sought. It had seemed too good to be true, meaning it probably was. It was why he'd hesitated before agreeing to the offer.

All he had to do was pay off a few debts? He would make her a fair offer to help repay some of what this lord had frittered away in gambling debts and bad investments. He would recoup the amount once he established the right connections.

Perhaps he had been overwhelmed by gratefulness. Or maybe he was looking for an excuse to kiss her before their relationship became contractual, for then this would be off-limits.

Whatever the reason, the longer she stood in front of him, the more he wanted her in his arms, to take her lips with his.

Her lips parted in shock when he leaned in toward her, and he felt the soft gasp as she breathed him in and their lips touched. She was still for a moment, and he almost pulled away. But then, she responded, moving beneath him, matching his subtle movements.

It was gentle, slow, and he knew that he should back away now, that this could be explained away if he stopped before this went any further.

But he had never been a man who stopped when he should have. He always took the extra step, didn't mind the risk, and was almost always rewarded.

Which was why he stepped forward, clasped his arm around her back, and hauled her up against him as his tongue parted her lips and he began to plunder.

Her moan caused a surge of lust to run straight through him to where he began to ache, as all he could focus on was her response to him, the way her tongue curled around his, inexperienced but eager. She pressed herself to him, her small breasts firm against his chest. He hadn't expected this. Not from her.

He'd had many women before, but never a lady.

The thought had him wrenching himself back away from her. This would only work without emotion or attachment. He doubted she could separate that from the physical.

What had he done?

She stood there appearing helplessly adrift, blinking up at him in shock, her lips red from his pressure. She was thoroughly disheveled, and it was entirely his fault. He ran a hand through his hair as he stepped backward as though he could escape this situation.

"My God, I am sorry," he said profusely. "I shouldn't have done that."

"No," she said, shaking her head as she pulled at her gown, straightening it before attempting to catch more of the stray tendrils of hair that had fallen loose. "You should not have."

Well, she certainly didn't appear to be a woman who was easily rattled.

"Do you… do you still want to go ahead with this?"

"Yes," she said resolutely, lifting her chin, and a flicker of fear ran through his chest as he wondered how much debt he was agreeing to take on. "It was just a kiss."

Just a kiss? If that was how she described what had just occurred between them, what kind of kisses had she had in the past? He had assumed she was a sheltered, inexperienced young lady. Had he misunderstood?

"Very well," he said. "Our last, then."

"Of course," she said with a nod. "We should return to the event. My father will be seeking me out."

She swept past him, an intoxicating scent of sweet cinnamon trailing behind her, his reaction catching him off guard for a moment until she stopped at the door and turned to him. "Perhaps you should wait a few minutes before following me in. But when you do, ask me to dance once the orchestra starts. We should begin building our story of how we met and were instantly drawn to one another. It must be believable."

She was calculating. Formidable. And, he noted as he accepted her direction, awe-inspiring.

For the first time he could remember, he couldn't wait to see what the Christmas season might hold.

CHAPTER 4

*O*nce she turned the corner, out of sight of the alcove, Noelle stopped and placed a hand on her chest, covering her racing heart.

Not only had she practically proposed to a man she hardly knew, but he had accepted – and then had kissed her. A life-altering kiss that she wasn't sure she could ever recover from. She hoped she had been successful in not showing him just how affected she had been, but she wasn't sure how she would spend the next two months in his presence without thinking of his lips on hers yet again.

Damn the man.

She should have known to expect the unexpected from someone like him.

But here they were.

Not only that but now she had to dance with him – and provide an explanation of their connection to her father.

Eventually, she recovered well enough to return to the assembly rooms, where she smiled and nodded and made the inconsequential talk that she hated with various members of the *ton* until she saw him again.

As though sensing her stare, he met her eye across the room, and unlike most people, he didn't drop his gaze at being caught – nor did she. He held her stare, and he slowly, deliberately winked at her.

Causing additional turmoil in her belly.

He held her stare as he turned away from his conversation – which would have been considered the height of rudeness, but he didn't seem to care – and stalked across the room toward her. Noelle couldn't have said what the musicians were playing, so focused was she on the man who now stood before her. He reached down, took her hand, and lifted it upward, kissing her knuckles.

"Lady Noelle. You look beautiful this evening."

Did he mean that?

"Thank you," she said, hoping he couldn't tell how affected she was. One damn kiss, and she had lost all of the reason she always so prided herself on.

"Would you care to dance?"

"I would like that very much," she said, allowing him to lead her to the dance floor.

As he placed one hand on her waist and took the other in his grasp, she belatedly realized the dance.

"You waited until a waltz," she said accusatorily, and he smiled broadly as he lifted a brow.

"Of course I did. You told me to sell the story of our romance, did you not? What point would it make if I asked you to dance in a set in which I would hardly be speaking to you?"

"It is not the speaking part that concerns me."

"What is it, then? How close I might hold you?" he said as he tugged her toward him until their bodies were nearly flush.

"People will talk," she said, trying to shift backward, but he held her firm, and the truth was, she rather liked it.

25

"Isn't that the point?"

"The point is to sell our engagement, not scandal."

He shrugged. "Every aspect of my life would scandalize most people here."

"Should I be concerned?"

"You chose me, my lady," he said mockingly, and she nodded.

"I know." She cleared her throat before continuing. "I will have to tell my father about our *engagement*. I wish I could tell him the truth, but he would be too likely to give it away. I will have to concoct a story for him."

"Tell him we met here and that I was so taken with you that I could not help but pursue you."

"If we tell him you'll cover his debts, he likely will not care much."

His gaze upon her hardened. "He is more concerned about his financial situation than his daughter?"

Noelle wasn't sure if she was more defensive of her father or appreciative that Mr. Hartwell would evidently care about her in this short time that they had known one another.

"He is concerned that he will no longer be able to find an appropriate marriage for me."

"Would he consider me appropriate?"

"In the past, no." She didn't see the point in lying. "Now, he might be more open to a man without a title if such a man can provide for me."

"Very well. I will be my most charming self when I call on you tomorrow."

"Tomorrow?"

"Yes. No time like the present, is there? Then we can begin on these invitations you mentioned."

Right. That was the reason he had agreed to this, she reminded herself. As he swept her across the floor, his strong hand splayed across her back, her stomach pressed against

26

him, and her hand interlocked with his. It was easy to forget what had brought them together. He didn't actually have any interest in her besides what her name and social standing could offer him.

Do not be a fool, Noelle, she told herself. He is a means to an end. This was a business proposition on both sides.

"What is the matter?" he asked, and she shook herself from her thoughts.

"There is no matter."

"Your face says you're lying."

"All is well, Mr. Hartwell."

"Call me Cooper."

"That is rather informal."

"If you were going to be my wife, I would not have you call me Mr. Hartwell. Can you imagine being in bed together, calling out such a name?"

She swatted his shoulder. "Do not speak like that."

"Why not?" he asked, his lips quirked in amusement.

Because it made her think of things she had no business thinking of. Because she hated how much she *liked* the thought of the two of them lying in bed together. Because if he continued, he would make it very hard to agree to all the terms of their contract.

"Because it is not appropriate."

"Lady Noelle, I didn't realize you were such a prude. Not after our... interlude."

She snorted. "I do not believe I played any part in that."

"Oh, I distinctly remember the role you played," he said, and as he grinned at her, she was so caught in the dimple that appeared in his cheek beneath his slight stubble that she hadn't realized the music had stopped until he came to a standstill himself.

"Until tomorrow," he said, and before she could offer a retort, he bowed briefly and then slipped away.

Leaving her wondering just what she had gotten herself into.

* * *

COOPER HAD NEVER CALLED upon a woman before.

He most certainly had never called upon a young lady.

Nor had he ever imagined he would be at the door for the daughter of a viscount.

He'd had to ask around to find out when he should arrive. It seemed that morning, when he was most productive, was unacceptable, but that morning calls occurred mid-afternoon.

Ridiculous.

Nevertheless, he knew he would have to make some sacrifices if he would see this through, so here he was.

He had asked one of his men of business to find the address for him, and he hoped that Lord Walters would be at home, in addition to Lady Noelle herself.

He shook his head as he tried to forget her red, irresistibly kissable lips, the glint in those warm brown eyes, and her mischievous expressions as she tried not to let him know what she was thinking.

But he had been able to tell – very much so.

She had been uncertain what they had agreed to, but his kiss had rattled her, as much as she had tried to hide it from him.

He wanted to know more about her, but he was worried that doing so would give the wrong impression.

This was business.

His knock took some time to answer. Finally, a harried maid opened the door to him. The lack of a butler informed him that the family was harder off than Lady Noelle had alluded to last night. Not only that but as the maid led him

28

through the first two rooms, it was clear that most of the house was devoid of furniture. Lady Noelle and Lord Walters were either leaving this London house, or Lord Walters had been forced to sell most of their belongings.

Neither was a good sign.

"Mr. Hartwell – Cooper. You're here."

There she was, standing in the entrance of the front room, which he guessed was supposed to be a drawing room based on the one sofa that still sat within it.

"I told you I would be here. I am a man of my word," he said instead of greeting her. He found it best to go directly to the point.

"So it seems," she said before gesturing to the sofa. "Please sit. I apologize that we do not have much to offer. We are currently preparing to leave our London house. After Lady Burton's house party, we will continue to our country estate."

"Will you return to London?"

She didn't meet his gaze. "We shall see."

He sat back, crossing one leg over the other as he studied her, where she sat on the other end of the sofa, slightly turned away from him.

"Your father is in worse debt than you said."

"He is," she agreed.

"What is to say that he won't return to debt once this is complete?"

"Nothing, I suppose," she said dejectedly. "As much as I wish to say that he has learned from his past, he is also easily swayed."

"Well, hopefully I can *sway* him to accept me as a son-in-law."

She nodded, leaning forward and passing him a piece of paper she had clutched between her fingers.

"I created our contract. I have no problem if you want to take it and read it in detail before signing it."

29

He eyed her from over the top of the paper before leaning back and holding it out in front of him. She seemed surprised when he slipped glasses out of his pocket and placed them on his nose.

"I am nearly perfect. Not quite," he said with a grin as she rolled her eyes.

He quickly scanned the page, hiding his surprise at all it revealed.

"Did you write this yourself?"

"I did," she said defensively.

"It is well done."

"I have reviewed many contracts for my father," she said, a blush stealing up her cheeks along with a touch of pride.

"I see," he said, nodding. "The amount your father owes is considerable."

"It is."

"If I am going to provide you with your requested amount, then I must ask for more on your end."

"More?" her eyes flashed. "What else could there be? I told you that I will not—"

He held up a hand. "I would never ask a woman to give herself to me unwillingly or as part of a business deal. Besides, you've already included that subject as discussed in the contract and I will not amend it, for it would cause too much conflict when we part ways. What I would ask is that at least one business dealing comes out of all of your introductions."

Her mouth gaped open. "I cannot guarantee a contract. All I can provide is connections."

"Yes, but I need to ensure you tell everyone how wonderful I am. Help me to appear more than acceptable even though I was not born into a noble family."

"You appear well educated. You must have had a decent upbringing."

"I went to a ragged school for a few years but am mostly self-taught. I am still a commoner, and that will never change – even if I did marry you."

"Which you will not."

"I will not."

Somehow during their exchange, the space between them had closed, until now only inches separated their faces.

Cooper couldn't wrench his eyes away from her, so focused were they on her pert, upturned nose, her beautiful red lips with that little crease in the middle, and the crinkle at the corner of her eyes that told him she was a woman who smiled often.

He was leaning toward her again, nearly repeating the unacceptable when a voice cut through the door.

"Noelle? Do we have a visitor?"

He tore his eyes away to provide his attention upon the man standing in the doorway. The man who was, for all intents and purposes, going to become his future father-in-law.

"Lord Walters," he said, turning on his charm. "Just the man I want to see."

"Cooper Hartwell?" the man bit out, his baffled expression turning to one of concern. "What are you doing with my daughter?"

He would like to do quite a few things with the man's daughter – but none of that would come true, let alone be put into words.

"Well, my lord," he said with a large smile, "I would like to marry her."

CHAPTER 5

 *wo months later*

THE CARRIAGE ROLLED to a stop in front of the grand estate. It had not been a long drive from the train station in Guilford, which was a few hours from London by rail, but Noelle had packed for three weeks, for they no longer had a London home to return to, despite the initial funds that Cooper had provided her.

She requested an amount upfront and the remainder once their business was concluded.

Business.

That would have to be on the forefront of her mind over the next few weeks – and not the man himself.

Noelle stole a glance toward him from the corner of her eye. She had seen him only occasionally since the day he appeared at their London townhouse and announced to her father that he would like to marry her.

Her father had been taken aback, for sure. Still, once

Cooper had announced how he had completely fallen for her and was willing to do all it took – most significantly, pay off any debts for his future wife's family instead of expecting a dowry – her father had quickly agreed.

There had been two more public engagements where they had both appeared, but this would be the first event with only titled guests that he had been welcome to. Lady Burton had been somewhat hesitant, but Hattie had insisted that they both attend and how could they turn away the man who Noelle was going to marry?

The short carriage ride from the train station in Guilford had been silent, her father and Cooper not having much to say to one another. Noelle supposed that her father's pride had taken a bit of a hit that his daughter was essentially being bought rather than he paying a dowry for her, but he hadn't left himself with much choice, now, had he?

The carriage door opened now, and a shock of cold wind blasted within. Noelle shivered as she shifted the carriage blanket off her legs. Cooper reached out and took it from her, the back of his hand brushing against hers as he did, the action warming her even though their touch was through her winter gloves, while his hands were bare.

She was reminded of how strikingly handsome he was each time she saw him. As much as she had tried to tell herself to be unaffected by his presence, it wasn't easy when he was so alluring. His mysterious past only added to his attraction.

He stood, first descending the stairs, before reaching up a hand and helping her out. She smiled in thanks, surprised when he held his elbow out for her.

"Fiancée," he murmured, reminding her that this is where the charade truly began.

They walked up the grand estate's stairs, the gravel crunching beneath their feet. Noelle's heart raced as they approached the imposing double doors flanked by intricate stone statues of mythical creatures. The door swung open before them, revealing a grand foyer adorned with towering evergreen trees, their branches twinkling with lit candles and delicate glass ornaments.

Lord and Lady Burton stood at the entrance, their faces alight with welcoming smiles that faltered slightly when their eyes ran over Cooper.

Noelle's father greeted their hosts warmly while Cooper nodded respectfully. Hattie, a vision in a rich crimson gown, hovered in the background with a curious glint in her eye as she watched Noelle and Cooper.

She wished she could tell Hattie everything, but she remembered one of the stipulations of her contract—that no one would know the truth. Hattie's sister, Hermione, joined her a moment later, her flushed cheeks matching her dress.

"Welcome to Burton Manor," Lady Burton said, her voice as elegant as her surroundings. "We are delighted to have you join us for our Christmas house party."

A rush of nervous excitement tore through Noelle as she took in the opulent surroundings. The walls were draped with sumptuous fabrics, the air filled with the irresistible scent of evergreen and spiced cider. Servants bustled about, preparing for the evening's festivities, their footsteps muffled by the plush carpets that lined the halls.

This was what it would be like to live in a house where one could afford to keep servants and host lavish parties, although Noelle couldn't say she found a particular draw to doing so.

She looked beside her, wondering if Cooper was the type of man who would expect to host such gatherings. Likely, if it meant increasing his precious business connections.

Not that it mattered – for she would never actually be his wife.

As they were led through the manor and briefly introduced to some of the other house guests, Noelle couldn't help but notice the whispers that followed in their wake. She caught snatches of conversation from passing guests, their curious and judgmental gazes lingering a moment too long on Cooper.

He didn't need an introduction – everyone already knew who he was.

She was surprised by her surge of protectiveness towards him, knowing he was out of his element. But she also couldn't deny the thrill that accompanied the realization that they were embarking on this adventure together – that neither of them was alone in this.

"We shall show you to your rooms, and then you must join us for dinner," Lady Burton said. "Most of the other guests have already arrived."

She handed them off to a housekeeper who murmured, "Follow me." Noelle kept her arm fully wrapped around Cooper's as they ascended the staircase. Her father was first shown to his room. The housekeeper continued down a corridor until she came to a stop. "Yours, my lady," she said, gesturing to one door before pointing across the hall. "And yours, my—sir."

"Thank you," Cooper said warmly despite her error, and Noelle couldn't help but ask a question that had been weighing on her mind since she had first overheard him talking to his brother.

"Do you truly want to be a part of this world?" she asked, to which he smirked and shook his head.

"Who would ever desire to be noble?" he scoffed. "It is a necessity to *use* this world, Noelle. Not a desire."

She hated that she loved how her name sounded on his lips, how he rounded the O, and his voice dropped when he said it – even when he was essentially reminding her of how he was using *her*.

"Well," she said, needing to break the tension between them before it could harden. "I shall see you at dinner?"

"Of course," he said before stepping into his doorway, tilting his head over the oak door to peer at her. "You know where to find me if you need me before then."

She could still hear his laughter after he shut the door and continued into the room. What disconcerted her was that she could equally feel it, deep in her soul.

* * *

COOPER KNEW EXACTLY what and who he would be encountering when he arrived at this party.

Not the names of each guest but the type of people themselves.

"Why do you not tell me the names of everyone in attendance again to see if you remember them?" Noelle asked as they walked down the staircase together. She didn't realize he only needed to be told something once to remember it.

"Lord Bingly, Lady Crupley, her daughter Lady Brighton, Lord and Lady Aster, their daughter Lucy, and their son John—"

"Lord John," she interjected, holding up a figure. "He is very particular on the 'Lord'."

"Of course he would be," Cooper scoffed. "Very well, *Lord* John."

"This is what you are getting yourself into," she warned, and he nodded.

"Of course. Lord Rochester and his brother, Lord Andrew. Lord Northbridge and his sister, Lady Jennifer. Then our hosts, Lord and Lady Burton, their daughters

Hattie and Hermione, and their son, Lord Leopold, who is away on the continent."

As he spoke, he couldn't stop running his eyes over her.

Her lips were as red as they had been earlier in the day, and he couldn't help but wonder if he kissed her again, would the rouge come off, or were her lips naturally that color?

Her gown matched her lips. The bodice was fitted with a high neckline adorned with a lace collar. The sleeves were long, with delicate lace cuffs peeking out near her fingers. The bodice featured intricate embroidery that appeared to be twigs of greenery.

The skirt was full and floor-length, not as volumized as the dresses many of the ladies would be wearing, but from what he had seen, Noelle preferred simpler garments.

"Holly," she said, following his gaze to the gown's embroidery, her cheeks reddening again in her most becoming way. "My mother loved Christmas. I try to honor that."

He wanted to ask so much more, but they were not yet well enough acquainted for him to know if she would be averse to jests about her name. He supposed she might take it to heart if it had been her mother who had loved the holiday.

"There you are!" Lady Hattie said, practically bounding up toward them when they reached the bottom of the staircase. After one relatively suspicious look toward Cooper, she lowered her voice as she looked surreptitiously around her and then leaned in toward Noelle. "Mother insisted I speak with the Rochester twins, and they are both falling all over themselves to try to impress me."

"I would be too," Noelle said with a smile for her friend. "Lady Hattie, I am not certain if you have met Mr. Hartwell?"

"You will know my mother, of course, Mr. Hartwell, as she is the one always trying to separate you from your money," Hattie said, eliciting a chuckle from Cooper. "I hope

I am not rude in saying, however, that I was surprised to hear of your quick engagement."

"It was rather quick, Hattie, I know," Noelle said, and Cooper felt a moment of guilt that he had asked her to keep this a secret from even her closest friends. But the circle must be kept tight. "I wish I had time to tell you of it before the party, but we were only just becoming acquainted, and you had already left for the country. Mr. Hartwell and I met at your mother's charity ball."

"I do recall seeing you dance."

"It was surprising to both of us how quickly we fell for one another."

The words rolled off of her tongue, surprising Cooper. He wasn't aware she would tell the stories so easily, but they had practiced this before.

"Well, I am happy for you, Noelle, of course," she said with a small smile.

"Thank you, Lady Hattie. That means more to me than you know," Cooper said sincerely. He wasn't certain that all would greet him with such a warm welcome, but he knew it would mean a lot to Noelle for one of her closest friends to be accepting.

"Tell me, Hattie," said Noelle, "is there anyone here you would *like* to charm? Besides the Rochester twins?"

"Perhaps Lord Northbridge," Lady Hattie said shyly.

"Lord Northbridge it is, then," Cooper said enthusiastically, for Lord Northbridge would be an acquaintance of importance. "Nothing like the present."

They steered around a few guests with polite nods before Noelle led them to the corner, where the man in question was currently chattering.

On their way, he couldn't notice how more heads began to turn toward them, and the whispers began. Let them. It wasn't anything new.

They stopped in front of two gentlemen, and when it seemed that Noelle was not inclined to say anything, Cooper decided to start the conversation.

"What brings you here to Burton Manor, Lord Northbridge?" Cooper said before Noelle suddenly began to speak.

"Lord Northbridge and Lord John, might I please introduce my betrothed, Mr. Cooper Hartwell?"

"Ah, yes," Lord Northbridge said, a slight gleam in his eye as he somewhat ignored Cooper, although that was not unexpected. "I heard that you were engaged." His eyes flicked up and down over Cooper. "A pity."

"A pity?" she repeated, and Cooper couldn't help but step forward. While many noblemen had become used to aligning themselves with people who had acquired their wealth outside land ownership, that didn't mean they were all pleased about it. Cooper was used to being looked down upon, but that didn't mean Noelle had to bear the weight of it. He had to be careful to walk the line of demanding respect while not ostracizing himself.

"I believe, Lady Noelle, he means that it is a pity you are no longer available as an eligible young lady." Cooper looked down his nose at Lord Northbridge, daring him to suggest differently. "Is that not what you were insinuating?"

Lord Northbridge, it seemed, was not one to back down.

"Actually," he said, stepping toward Cooper until they were nearly toe-to-toe, "that is not what I meant, nor is it up to you to make any assumptions."

"Why don't you tell me, then?"

"I *meant* that it is a pity that Lady Noelle is engaged to a commoner. I could hardly believe that Walters would stoop so low."

Cooper opened his mouth to respond, but he was surprised when a gentle hand rested on his arm, and Noelle stepped between them.

39

"Lord Northbridge," Noelle said, standing tall, her shoulders squared back. "My fiancé was invited here, just as you were. I would ask that you be polite to him and to me. Mr. Hartwell might not have been born into the same set of circumstances as you or I, but the fact that he has made such a great success of himself is sure to be admired, is it not?"

Lord Northbridge clearly wanted to say more, his nostrils flaring as he pressed his lips tightly together.

"Yes, Lady Noelle, you are correct," he finally managed.

She stood still, waiting, and Cooper had to work hard to prevent his laughter from emerging.

Finally, she won the battle of wills as Lord Northbridge succumbed.

"It is wonderful to meet your acquaintance, Mr. Hartwell," he muttered through tight lips. "I do hope you enjoy your stay."

"Thank you, Lord Northbridge," Cooper said with enthusiasm. "I am sure I shall, with such excellent company."

"Lady Hattie, we are happy to see Lord Northbridge, are we not?" Noelle said, drawing her friend, who had remained silent throughout the exchange, forward between them as Lord John melted away, apparently finding this confrontation too much to bear.

"As I am you," Lord Northbridge said, his countenance softening. "Always a pleasure."

Lady Hattie nodded, but she no longer seemed so inclined to charm Lord Northbridge as she had been previously. Perhaps she hadn't realized that the man's true colors did not shine as brightly as she had thought.

"I look forward to seeing you at dinner," she said, beginning to back away when Lord Northbridge stepped forward and took her elbow.

"We appear to be standing beneath the mistletoe," he said, looking overhead. Cooper followed his gaze but saw only a bough from one of the Christmas trees their hosts had placed throughout the room.

"I believe you are mistaken, my lord," he murmured, earning him a curious glance from Lady Hattie.

"We are going to help with the decorations tomorrow," Hattie murmured. "Perhaps, then, the mistletoe will be placed around the house."

Which would be up for everyone to find or ignore.

As for Cooper, he knew that it would be something he should try hard to avoid – even if a part of him wanted nothing more than to be trapped beneath it with Noelle.

CHAPTER 6

"Welcome, everyone, to our home and the beginning of what is sure to be the most fabulous Christmas party."

Lord Burton was standing at the head of the table, pontificating about the Christmas season. It was all noise to Noelle, who couldn't help sneaking a look next to her at Cooper, wondering what he thought of all this pomp. She was sure he disdained it as a man who was much more inclined to do everything with purpose, but then, he was the one who had desired integration in this life.

So here he was.

A small smile played on the edge of his lips. She was sure he was attempting to be friendly, but part of her also wondered whether he was silently mocking all of the circumstance.

The interaction with Lord Northbridge had been dreadful. Noelle had been embarrassed, not by Cooper but rather by the other guests, who were part of a group she was born into, even if she wasn't always pleased with how they acted.

She had spoken up before she'd had time to think about

what she was doing, but she was prepared to defend her words repeatedly if Lord Northbridge had anything more to say. At least Cooper had seemed appreciative. Maybe he would be inclined to drop the stipulations to their agreement that a business deal needed to come from her introductions. It was a ridiculous item, which she had told him.

He agreed to the upfront amount regardless of what happened, but the final amount would only come if the situation ended as he wanted.

Typical, she huffed, crossing her arms over her chest as she was annoyed by it anew, earning herself a nudge from his elbow.

"Something amiss?" he murmured in her ear, his voice low and throaty, strumming a wanting deep in her core.

"No," she said, shaking her head and dropping her arms, telling herself not to wear her emotions so outwardly around a man who seemed to notice more than most. "All is well."

"Tell me if it's not," he said, and she nodded as Lord Burton finally stopped talking and raised his wine glass in a toast. Not having been paying attention, Noelle had no idea to what they were toasting, but she assumed that it had something to do with the season.

"To Christmas together," Cooper echoed the rest of the group, holding his glass up to Noelle. She was surprised, at first thinking he was referring to the two of them, before realizing it was the toast the entire party was engaging in.

"To Christmas together," she murmured, only she wasn't speaking of the house party.

She meant this Christmas, between her and Cooper. She wasn't a fool. She knew that between a broken engagement and her father's loss of everything he owned, her chances of ever finding a husband were small.

So perhaps, even though there was no substance to this

betrothal, she would enjoy being one half of a partnership and pretend that this was true – for herself.

Cooper looked over at her, meeting her eyes, and she knew that he understood her meaning – even if he didn't feel it himself.

The rest of the dinner was course after course of lavish dishes, which Noelle knew was partly for celebration and partly to show just how prosperous Lord and Lady Burton were. First came baked oysters, then turtle soup served with bread rolls. This was followed by roast beef as the meal's centerpiece, along with pheasant that was likely caught on this very estate. A whole roasted trout and sides of mashed potatoes, parsnips, Brussels sprouts, and the richest of gravies, sauces, and redcurrant jellies were also served.

Cooper was practically moaning beside her when the mince pies, fruits, and jellies were produced for desserts. He rolled his head to the side to look at her.

"How do you all possibly eat this much night after night?" he asked, to which she lightly laughed.

"I only eat a few bites each course," she said. "Otherwise, I could never fit into my stays."

Realizing she had just spoken to him about her undergarments, she clapped her hand over her mouth, but he didn't seem to mind as he laughed easily, something he seemed to do often.

"I have learned my lesson. What did you most enjoy tonight?"

She blinked at him. No one had ever asked her that before. Come to think of it, no one had ever asked her much about what she cared for, liked, or disliked. Everyone always assumed that she liked what was placed in front of her. She didn't have much other choice.

"Ah… I suppose the oranges and pears and jellies," she said, her cheeks warming. "I have a bit of a sweet tooth."

"The very best kind," he said with a wide smile. He lifted a pear from his plate and placed it on hers. "There you are. One more of your favorites."

"But *you* must try it!" she insisted. "They are so good."

He ignored her protests as he leaned over, cut into the fruit with his fork, and lifted it to her lips.

"A bite," he said, and she nodded, her eyes captured and lost in his navy depths as he stretched the fork toward her.

"Mmm," she said, her eyes closing along with her lips over the pear. When she opened her eyes and met his stare, she was shocked at how they had darkened, his pupils widening as he stared at her.

"What is the matter?" she asked, and he blinked a few times before backing away.

"Nothing," he muttered, suddenly quite concerned with his napkin as he pushed himself back slightly from the table and took a sip from the sherry that had been brought out with dessert.

She shrugged, accepting that she might never understand him.

And that was fine – because they were not meant to be together.

* * *

COOPER HAD NEARLY ALLOWED himself to be captivated by his fake bride once again. What was it about the woman?

She should be like any other young lady, but he was beginning to learn that she was far from it. She had depth and substance. She was more.

Not long after the dessert course was cleared, the senior women at the table stood, followed by the rest of the young ladies.

"We will be retiring to the drawing room for a time,"

Noelle said lowly to him, as though she wasn't entirely sure whether he would know the customs, but he was well aware of this. "I shall see you after."

"Not to worry," he said, patting her hand. "I shall be just fine on my own."

He placed a hand over his mouth to hide his chuckle as she followed the other women out of the room. He appreciated she was doing her best to look after him, but he had come far enough in this world alone. He could handle these gentlemen just fine without her.

Lord Walters was the first to sit beside him as the footman poured brandy and passed out cigars.

Northbridge and the little "Lord John," as he must be called, seated themselves as far from him as possible, as though he might infect them with his inferiority.

"Burton always has the finest drinks and cigars," Walters said conspiratorially. "Be sure to indulge."

"I feel as though I've already done too much of that," he said with a laugh.

Walters nodded ruefully, inhaling his cigar long before leaning back and taking a closer look at Cooper.

"We haven't had much chance to talk, the two of us, have we?"

"No," Cooper said cautiously, wondering where this was going.

"My daughter... she is a good girl. Smart. Headstrong, perhaps too much so, but she knows what she wants and isn't afraid to go after it. She and her mother were the same. Both of them took care of me."

He sighed, sipping his drink, turning the glass between his fingertips before continuing.

"When her mother passed, we both took it hard, but Noelle recovered first, as she had promised her mother to look after me, and she took that promise seriously. Sometimes I worry as I don't know who will look out for her. Not that I've done a very good job of it lately anyway."

He lifted his head. "I need you to promise me that you will always take care of her no matter what happens. Be kind to her. Look out for her. Let her tell you what to do, as she will probably be right most of the time, but also be a guide."

Cooper's breath caught in his throat. He wanted to agree to what the man said, for he could tell how much it would mean to him to hear those words. But could he straight up lie to him? He would leave Noelle once this was all finished, and her father would know then that this was all a farce.

But he had promised Noelle that they would see this through, and this man had caused the debts that had put his daughter in this very position at having to do this.

"Yes, I will look after her," he promised, realizing as he said it that he meant it. The two of them might not marry, but he would ensure she was well. They could stay in touch if they could be friends, and he could check in on her now and again.

Even the thought that she would likely be married to another by then caused a strange sensation of jealousy to rise within him, one that had no right to be present in his stomach.

By the time they rejoined the ladies, he had looked forward to seeing her again. As he approached Noelle at the far side of the room, their hostess called for a game of Blindman's Bluff, and Cooper had to hide his eyes rolling.

A man in his position had no time to play games without purpose. Not when there were far more important games to be played. Games that meant keeping everyone fed and housed. But he had heard of such a game before, and it didn't take much intelligence to play it.

"Do you know the rules?" Noelle asked him quietly, and he raised a brow.

"Yes, I think I can figure it out," he said, as Lord John was named the blindman and a scarf was tied around his eyes.

"Would you rather we tour the house and escape this game?" she asked, sensing his chagrin.

"I would like that very much," he said with such relief that she laughed. When it came time for them to hide from the blindman, she nodded toward the other side of the room, and he followed as they slipped out the door together.

Noelle seemed to know where she was going, having been here previously, and he once again marveled at the display of wealth present in each room.

His holdings were likely not far from these, yet he didn't think he would ever feel such a need to display it as they did. He supposed it was because, for them, the reason to accumulate such riches was for the power it held, and part of that was prestige that must be flaunted to be respected.

He was glad he wasn't held to the same standard.

It provided him with a much greater sense of freedom.

Freedom that he wasn't willing to be rid of yet.

CHAPTER 7

"This is the orangery," Noelle said, leading Cooper through a door at the very back of the manor. The large room was attached to the house, yet the air was warm and humid. "Whenever I visit Burton Manor, I make it a point to spend time here – especially during the cooler months of the year."

Cooper followed her along the stone path, his neck craning to take in the various fruits that hung overhead. He reached up and plucked a pear off a tree before leaning down and tucking it into Noelle's pocket.

She swiftly inhaled when he leaned down close to her, but he backed away as quickly as he had hidden the fruit.

"How did you know where my pocket was?"

"Through the power of observation," he said with a wink, and her breath caught. He shouldn't be so charming if he wanted to keep this as a business arrangement. "How often have you joined the Burton family for Christmastide?"

"A few times. We usually celebrated on our estate, even though our family was so small. However, we would often come for an evening or two of celebration during the

Christmas season, and Hattie and I spent a lot of time together in the summer months. It was usually rather fun and worth the half-day ride."

"You said your mother enjoyed Christmas. Do you?"

She picked at the fabric of her skirt as she considered the question.

"I suppose I used to love Christmas as much as she did. She made it so magical when I was a child. There were always decorations and laughter and baking and all of the traditions that made Christmas such a special time. She took such care in her gifts for me, and we did everything together. When she passed… Christmas just lost that special spark that it had previously, even though I try to keep her memory alive. I wasn't sure if we should attend this year, but last year it was a rather lonely Christmas with just me and my father."

"What is it truly about for you?"

"Christmas?"

"Yes."

"I suppose the togetherness with people I love."

"So, this house party with me doesn't exactly count?" he said with a self-deprecating chuckle.

"My father is here, as is Hattie, one of my closest friends, and her sister, Hermione, although she is not nearly as sweet," she said, leaning back and looking at him. A lock of thick, dark hair had fallen over his eyes. She leaned up, pushing it back and away from his forehead.

He leaned into her touch, and she smiled at him, wondering if he had anyone close to him that he was missing this season. "Perhaps we could be friends as well."

"We could," he agreed, his eyes warm as the crinkles grew around the edges while he looked at her.

"What does Christmas mean to you?" she asked, and he looked away from her, into the distance through the glass panes of the orangery, although the grounds beyond were too dark to distinguish.

"Nothing, to be honest," he said. "My family was never particularly close. My father left us, and Trenton and I had to find a way to look after ourselves and my mother. She was always so overworked trying to provide for us that she was too exhausted to do much to make Christmas special. We would go to church, of course. Sometimes have a bit of a special meal or receive a trinket if she remembered."

"I'm sorry," Noelle said softly, feeling for him.

"Nothing to be sorry for," he said with a shrug. "It's just another day."

"Well, you are now at Burton Manor," she said wryly. "It will certainly be more than just another day. I'm sure you've had a taste of it so far."

"It hasn't been half bad," he admitted, looking down at her with one side of his mouth lifted, his hands clasped behind his back.

"I am glad to hear it," she said, wondering why she was so relieved when he had asked to be here.

"I have had excellent company," he said. "Especially this young woman who continues to defend my honor."

Noelle swung her head around to him in shock. "Do you mean me?"

"Who else would I mean?" He laughed. "I do appreciate what you said to Lord Northbridge, even though I can handle such a man, as I have done many times in the past."

"His countenance is embarrassing."

"That's on him, not on you."

"Yes, but—"

"I should not be blamed for the sins of all of the businessmen in London, do you not agree?" he asked with a pointed look.

"Of course." He was right. She had been placing undue blame upon herself.

"You and I are in this together. We should be fine if we can continue to look out for one another. Now tell me, how many blasted games will we be playing?"

Noelle sighed. "One most every night, I'm afraid."

"Well, I have been rather adept at games in my life, although most have been of far greater consequence," he said.

"You seem to know how to do it much better than my father," she said ruefully. "I do not know what he has been thinking lately."

"Grief can cause a person to make ill decisions," Cooper said. "I still do not believe *you* should bear the burden of his choices. Besides, we were both on the losing end in this recent case."

"I must admit that I was surprised to hear that you had also made a poor investment."

"Heard of me, had you?" He winked at her.

"I had heard of you, yes. Hasn't everyone in London?" she said, lifting a brow. "I couldn't help but wonder, though – why did you agree to it?"

"The men involved have had success before," he said. "It seemed like a sure thing. I was as shocked as anyone when they disappeared with the money."

"Where would they go?" Noelle asked. "Is it that easy for a man to simply disappear?"

"I suppose if one truly doesn't want to be found," he said, staring rather intently at her before seemingly making up his mind about something. "If it means that much to you, however, I will make a few inquiries. See if anyone has heard anything about them. Would that help?"

"I would be very grateful," she said. "I know it seems small, but it would go a long way for a man like my father. Besides, I don't like the thought of someone escaping consequence after purposefully causing so much trouble for other people."

"You are a fair woman."

"Some would say I am vengeful," she said with a laugh.

"Not me," he responded. "I couldn't have gotten to where I am today if I wasn't fair."

"I understand," she said as they reached the end of the circular path around the orangery. The steaminess in the air seemed to permeate the space between them as Noelle felt her hair beginning to curl around her face. "We should probably return."

"We probably should," he agreed.

Except she had enjoyed this time with him far more than she would have if she were playing Blindman's Bluff. Not that she could ever admit that.

They stopped in front of the doors, facing one another.

"Thank you for the tour of the orangery," he said, dipping his head, and Noelle had a strange wish that he would lean down and kiss her.

But he wouldn't. He couldn't. Nor was it something she should have been contemplating.

Instead, she turned and reached for the door handle at the same time that he did. Their hands touched, and she jerked hers back as though she had been burned while he murmured, "Allow me," and turned the knob.

Only it didn't turn.

It stuck.

He tried the other way, but it still didn't move.

"Is it locked?" she asked, looking up at him with a frown. "How could that be?"

"The orangery appears to have been added onto the house during its history, so I am sure this was an exterior door at one point. This was no accident." He met her gaze. "Someone locked us in."

* * *

"It could not have been purposeful," Noelle said, pursing her lips together, the expression on her face one that Cooper well recognized. She was trying to solve their current problem, already moving on from what had caused it.

Cooper was still concerned about that part of it. He could admit to being an overly suspicious man. One had to be when faced with so many adversaries. And yet, in this, he wondered if someone had a reason to prevent them from returning to the party.

"Did anyone know we were out here?" he asked, and Noelle shook her head.

"I didn't think we should inform anyone where we were going. Even though we are betrothed, I should still have a chaperone if we are alone together."

"I never thought of that," he said, dread filling him at the idea. If he had to spend weeks following all of these rules, it better be worth it at the end. And if they were caught alone without proper supervision, would it mean that this brief arrangement would become something much more permanent?

"You do not think someone meant to trap us out here, do you?" she asked as she picked up on his suspicions. The woman had natural intuition. She would do well in his world if she were a man.

However, he was pleased with his choice of woman, for she would be well-suited to help him with his current endeavors.

"I cannot see one of the servants locking the doors before everyone retired for the night," he said. "It feels too contrived, although I cannot understand why. But we will have to worry about that later. First, we must escape before we end up here all night."

"Scandal on the first night of a Christmas house party might not attract the proper notice."

He nodded before his attention moved to the top of her head as he searched within the auburn strands.

"Are you interested in how I have styled my hair tonight?" she asked suddenly, and he chuckled.

"I am, actually," he said, leaning toward her, hearing the catch in her breath as he lifted his hand and reached behind her ear, surprising her when he slipped a pin out without her even noticing until she saw it in his hand and a curl dangled much lower over her ear.

"What are you doing?" she said, her voice not much louder than a whisper.

"Getting us out of here."

He returned to the doorknob, kneeling before it and slipping the pin into the lock.

"Do you know how to unlock it without a key?"

"I have done this a few times," he murmured as he tried to concentrate. "It just might take some time."

"Is there anything I can do to help?"

"Just wait."

He closed his eyes, allowing himself to feel what was required rather than force the lock. He turned the pin a few times until he finally felt the click as he turned the lock simultaneously.

"Were you a thief in another life?" she asked, and he bristled, unsure just how he was supposed to respond. When he opened his eyes and met hers, he realized that she was joking, and his smile began to spread. If only she knew.

He turned the handle – and the door slid open before them.

He lifted his hand to her with one foot on the floor and the other kneeling beneath him.

"Well, shall we?" he said.

She placed her hand on his.

"We shall."

Cooper was on edge as they neared the drawing room where they had left the remainder of the party, wondering if anyone present had contrived against him.

"Be watchful," he murmured from the corner of his lips to Noelle, for that was precisely what he would do – be on the hunt for any surprised responses when the two of them appeared.

It didn't seem he was going to get his wish, however, for when they walked into the room, it appeared that some of the guests had already retired while a few of the gentlemen were gathered in the corner in what appeared to be a serious conversation. They all looked their way when they entered the drawing room, and an expression of ire, not surprise, flashed across Lord Northbridge's face.

Cooper was just going to have to keep his guard up – not what he was expecting during the Christmas season at the home of a nobleman. But it seemed that not much was changing in his life.

Not at the moment, anyway.

CHAPTER 8

"*G*ood morning!" Lady Burton said, walking into the breakfast room the next day, her hands clasped in front of her. "Who is ready to decorate?"

It seemed this was when and where she presented the day's itinerary.

The buffet spread that covered the table at the side of the room was likely enough to feed an entire village, and Noelle had wondered just what to expect for the day ahead as there was always something extravagant planned at Lady Burton's house parties. It seemed she was about to find out.

"As you have all noticed, we have decorated the manor with the most beautiful evergreen trees. I am sure that if our queen visited, she and her husband would be most delighted!"

Lady Burton clapped her hands together eagerly, and Noelle wondered whether she truly thought there was a chance that Queen Victoria might deem their house party grand enough to visit.

"Have they left any for the forest?" Cooper murmured beside her, hiding his question as he brought his coffee to his lips, causing a laugh to bubble out of Noelle, one she had to cough to cover.

Lady Burton shot them an arched eyebrow that told them she was not amused, even if she hadn't heard his barb.

"We have a selection of decorations for you, including cranberry garlands, fruits, nuts, and baked cookies already strung. In the drawing room, we also set out paper and fabric if you want to make your own stars or angels!"

Noelle felt Cooper would not be altogether pleased about spending his day crafting, but it seemed he had learned his lesson for now and didn't have any more comments.

He carried a cup of coffee with him and followed Noelle out of the breakfast room and toward the drawing room. Noelle scanned the guests to determine who she could help Cooper become more familiar with.

Spying the Rochester twins, Noelle strategically chose a seat beside them, although both gentlemen were currently focused on Lady Crupley and her daughter, Brighton. She was a beauty and enjoyed flirtations, but Noelle had never known her to be serious about any gentlemen, despite her mother's intentions. Noelle picked up some of the fabric on the table before her, passing some over to Cooper, who accepted it but laid it on his leg, apparently having no intentions of doing any of the work.

"Lord Rochester?" she said, momentarily unsure which one was the elder, for they were nearly identical.

"Yes?" one of them turned to her, and she smiled.

"It is so lovely to see you here. It has been a time, has it not?"

"It certainly has, Lady Noelle," he said with a grin, his eyes crinkling in the corners. Noelle wasn't sure that either of the twins had ever spoken much more than a sentence at a time of a serious matter. They were far more interested in the next prank they were about to play.

"I wonder," she said, leaning forward as the other, Lord Andrew, seemed interested enough to join their conversation for the moment. "Have you planned your great prank for this year's house party?"

"Prank!" Lord Rochester exclaimed, placing a hand on his chest as though she had seriously wounded his character. "You believe that my brother and I would carry out a *prank*?"

She rolled her eyes as she placed a hand on Cooper's knee.

"I told my fiancé about what you did last time I attended a party here at Burton Manor, but he wouldn't believe me. Perhaps you could tell him, for you are a much more adept storyteller."

The twins leaned forward, eyeing Cooper as though deeming whether he would be worthy.

"Lord Rochester and Lord Andrew, this is Mr. Hartwell," she said, squeezing his knee, and his lips curled up as though she had instructed them to at her touch. "I believe he would be a kindred soul, interested in learning more about your most inspired ideas."

"It is true," Cooper said with a nod. "I once devised a trick in which I created a large wire spider that I attached by thread to the back of a friend's shirt. By the time he realized that the spider only ran as fast as he did, we'd all had quite the laugh about it."

The twins exchanged a look with one another that allowed them some communication, for they both turned to Cooper as one and extended their hands.

"An excellent prank!" Lord Rochester said before Lord Andrew added, "Much admired!"

"Thank you," Cooper said modestly, crossing one leg over his other knee.

"Of course we are happy to tell you about last year," Lord Andrew said, leaning around his brother to better see Noelle and Cooper. Noelle leaned back into the sofa at Cooper's side as she began to work on stitching the fabric of her craft together, creating a small heart decoration while the men continued their discussion.

"Lord Burton loves his newspapers, as do most of the men, of course," Lord Andrew began, Lord Rochester, nodding his head, approving his brother's storytelling. The two began to trade sentences back and forth so quickly that Noelle found it challenging to keep track of who was saying what, for the two men spoke in such a way they were like one speaker.

"Before we left London, we wrote an entire newspaper about Lord and Lady Burton, their house party, and their guests and had a few copies printed."

"A few days into the Christmastide house party, we pilfered the real newspapers of the day from the butler and replaced them with ours."

"You can imagine Lord Burton's outrage when he began to read!"

The two men began to laugh, and Noelle couldn't help but smile as she remembered it. It had been a rather ingenious prank.

Cooper commended them, and the three began to trade stories back and forth. Noelle congratulated herself on another successful introduction. Still one deal to make and three weeks to do it. She wasn't sure how the Rochesters would be able to help him, but she supposed Lord Rochester might someday decide to do his duty and attend the House of Lords.

Or perhaps Cooper could invest in a prank store.

Soon enough, Lord Andrew's attention had returned to Lady Crupley's daughter, and Noelle had fashioned her heart ornament. She looked at Cooper's hands to find the fabric still lying there.

"Your decoration leaves much to be desired," she said wryly, and he passed the fabric to her.

"I am not exactly a 'decoration' type of man."

"So it would seem," she said before passing him her heart and fashioning a second out of his fabric. "I'll finish this, and then we can add a few things to a tree. Perhaps we will meet someone I can introduce you to while we walk there."

"Are any of these men influential?"

"Any of them with a title are. Even the men you just met on a substantial piece of land in Devon," she said. "You have never encountered any others in your business dealings?"

He shook his head, his jaw tight. "Not most of them, no. Most in this group of people stay far away from the likes of me."

"I see," she said quietly. "Hopefully this opportunity will change their minds."

When she finished, they stood together, deciding to go to the ballroom, where many trees stood.

"This is an odd tradition," Cooper mused, "cutting down trees to bring them inside to serve no purpose other than to stand in decoration."

"I agree," she said. "They have become quite the fashion among the nobility over the past few years now that Queen Victoria has made them popular. But they do smell beautiful and usher in a sense of the Christmas season. Lady Burton was one of the first to adopt the tradition."

"I feel Lady Burton would do anything that became in fashion, especially if the queen decreed it so."

"You are not wrong about that."

Four evergreens of various sizes stood in one corner of the ballroom. Lady Burton's actions were extreme, whether it was the number of parties and houseguests she invited, the courses she served for dinner, or the trees she cut down from their estate and brought indoors for Christmas.

They walked together to the front row of trees, and they saw a few of the other guests beginning to wander into the ballroom.

Noelle hung her heart on a tree, and Cooper hung his beside it. Noelle paused, noting the matching pair side by side.

"Well, if anyone happens by, they will certainly believe that we are together," Cooper said with a smile for her, and Noelle felt her real heart twitch unexpectedly.

Of course, his words were nothing more than a quip about their deal. Yet somehow, it hurt that he was so flippant about it.

Because they weren't together. Not now or ever.

"Did you discover anything about the lock last night?" Noelle asked in a low voice, needing to change the subject for herself.

"No," Cooper shook his head. "I asked the butler, however, and he said there was no reason for the door to have been locked before all of the guests were abed."

"So, it was purposeful."

"Apparently."

She looked at Northbridge, who walked by with a glare for both of them.

"Do you think it was him?" she whispered, and Cooper shrugged.

"He seems vindictive, and there was a discussion of consequence among the gentlemen last night. Perhaps there was something they wanted to keep me away from."

"I could ask my father."

"Don't," Cooper shook his head. "He and I are just becoming friendly. Wouldn't want my future father-in-law not to trust me for any reason."

She eyed him out of the corner of her eye. "He's not your future father-in-law."

"He doesn't know that – and neither does anyone else at this house party."

He smiled broadly at Lord Northbridge, who walked by with a smiling Hattie on his arm, her sister, Hermione, following with a smirk as she chatted to Lady Jennifer, Lord Northbridge's sister.

"Northbridge, how are you this morning?"

Lord Northbridge bristled, Cooper's intentions hitting their mark.

"It is *Lord* Northbridge."

"Ah, yes, my apologies. I forgot."

Cooper's grin was so large, and Lord Northbridge's ire grew so intense that Noelle couldn't help but diffuse the situation.

"Hattie, what decorations have you chosen?"

"My mother had some gilded decorations that I'd like to place on the trees," Hattie said shyly, even while Lord Northbridge seemed bored by the entire situation. "Lord Northbridge was kind enough to accompany me. Us," she added with a look back at Hermione.

"You could place them by our hearts," Noelle said, pointing to the tree beside them.

"How lovely," Hattie beamed. "You have always been so adept with a needle and thread, Noelle."

"Thanks to my mother," she said, noting then that Cooper and Lord Northbridge were eyeing one another with undisguised animosity.

"Well, I suppose we shall see you later tonight."

"Of course," Hattie said. "My mother will have another lavish dinner prepared. We are to dance tonight among these trees."

"We look forward to it," Noelle said, wrapping her hands around Cooper's elbow as she nudged him forward.

"Embarrassed of me?" he said wryly.

"Not at all," she said, shaking her head. "I just thought to avoid a brawl in the middle of Lady Burton's ballroom."

"Never," he scoffed, even though he looked away from her, proving she was right.

"You do like to provoke him."

"I can't stand assholes like that."

"Fair. But you wanted to be here. You don't have much choice."

"Perhaps not," he murmured before repeating, "perhaps not."

CHAPTER 9

*N*oelle successfully prevented Cooper and Lord Northbridge from spending time in one another's presence that evening. Fortunately, Lady Burton invited them all into the ballroom for a dance instead of retiring following dinner.

She had hired musicians from Guilford, a nearby village, so that none of the guests would miss out on the dancing.

"Here we are again," Cooper said as he led Noelle through the first set. She had grown somewhat used to his touch and was chagrined by how much she looked forward to the feel of his arms around her. She tried to tell herself that this was natural and that she was becoming comfortable with him from the time she spent with him, even though deep within, she was worried that there might be more to it.

His skill on the dance floor surprised her.

"Where did you learn to dance?" she asked as he moved her adeptly around the Christmas trees.

"When I determined the circles I needed to move in, I hired a tutor — for dance, among other skills."

That explained a lot.

"Well, it seems to have paid off."

"So it has."

The dance ended sooner than she liked, and Noelle found another gentleman standing before her.

"Lady Noelle, may I have this dance?"

Lord Northbridge.

She raised a brow, silently questioning his motive, but it wasn't something she could voice aloud.

"A dance with you?" Cooper said beside her, but Noelle placed a hand on his arm.

"All will be well," she said softly in his ear before turning to Lord Northbridge with a smile. "I would be happy to."

As Lord Northbridge led her onto the dance floor, she instantly noted the differences between him and Cooper – or perhaps it was just how she reacted to the two of them.

She welcomed Cooper's touch. She was comfortable with him. He was... well, he was like home.

Meanwhile, she was much more inclined to retreat from Lord Northbridge. He was cold and unrelenting. It was one of the reasons she had previously denied his suit.

"Tell me, Lady Noelle, what are you doing with a man like Hartwell?" he said, dispensing with any pleasantries.

"He is my betrothed, Lord Northbridge," she said politely. "I would ask — again — that you do not question me nor him or his character."

"I just asked why him," Lord Northbridge said with a shrug. "He is not a conventional choice."

"Many would say that I am an unconventional woman."

"Perhaps. But this is more than just an unconventional match. You are your father's only daughter."

If only he knew that the entire reason she was doing this was because of her father.

This was a country dance, which meant they switched partners for a time, giving Noelle a reprieve. When they returned, she tried not to say anything, hoping that they could conclude this dance and be done with it.

"Have you not considered any of the rest of us?"

He wasn't done.

"I did consider you once, Lord Northbridge," she said as firmly as she could. "I am happy with Mr. Hartwell. Please do not question it any longer. As we are on the topic, I would also appreciate you being more welcoming."

Lord Northbridge looked down his nose at her with a sneer. "Hartwell needs his woman to speak for him, does he?'

At that, Noelle had had enough. She had been raised to avoid scandal, as had most young women of her ilk, but she had also been raised by a mother who was as stubborn and outspoken as she was and had taught her not to allow anyone to speak down to her.

The dance broke, and she spun with her assigned partner since she wouldn't leave anyone alone. Anyone, that was, but Lord Northbridge. When it was time to return to him, she turned around and walked right out of the ballroom.

She heard his shout of annoyance from behind her, but she held her head high and continued walking. She didn't go to Cooper and didn't seek out her father. She didn't need anyone to stand up for her when she could do it perfectly fine herself. She wouldn't have Cooper looking out for her for much longer, so she might as well get used to defending herself.

When she entered the parlor beyond the ballroom, she hurried through, intending to make her way up the stairs and to her bedroom, pretending that she had a female emergency she had to see to.

She heard footsteps behind her, and she turned, ready for Cooper to have followed her out, her ire growing when she saw that it was Lord Northbridge.

"What do you think you are doing?" he hissed, his anger

high but his reserve preventing him from unleashing on her. "Leaving me in the middle of a set?"

"I had grown tired of your conversation," she said, not allowing him to evoke her ire. "I asked you politely not to speak of my engagement any longer, and you persisted."

"Because it makes no sense!" he exploded now, his restraint evaporated as he stormed into her space. She took a step back, holding up her hand. "You denied *me*!"

"Lord Northbridge, that was years ago. Please leave me be," she said sternly, which only angered him all the more.

"Who do you think you are, telling me what to do?" he said, his face so close to hers that she could smell the alcohol on his breath, and she recoiled. She had backed up so far that she met the wall behind her. He lifted an arm to trap her between him and the painting on the wall at her back. She tried to duck around him, but he held her fast.

"Lord Northbridge, you will remove your arm this moment!" she commanded, but he only narrowed his eyes at her.

"Or what?" he leered.

She was about to lift her knee and show him rather than tell him what she wanted him to do, but he suddenly disappeared from before her.

Instead, there was Cooper, standing over him, blood covering his fist from where it had met Lord Northbridge's nose.

* * *

WELL, so much for his invitation here.

Cooper knew the moment he withdrew his fist from Lord Northbridge's face that he had likely ruined all the opportunities he had created for himself at this house party and beyond.

But somehow, it was worth the resulting satisfaction. He had been watching Noelle dance with Northbridge, sensing her discomfort, but Lord John, of all people, had engaged him in conversation. Cooper hadn't been able to pass up the opportunity to speak with him further as this was one of the men he had come here specifically to connect with.

When he had returned his attention to the ballroom, he realized Noelle was no longer present but he had caught sight of Lord Northbridge storming past the Christmas trees and out the door, likely chasing after her.

When he saw Northbridge had trapped Noelle against the wall, Cooper lost all sense of reason.

"Cooper."

He heard Noelle, but her voice was distant, as though it was coming from another room and not right beside him.

"You hit me!" Northbridge moaned from the floor, and Cooper stooped down next to him so the man wouldn't forget his face.

"Yes. I did. The lady politely asked you multiple times to remove your arms – and your face – from her presence. You had ample opportunity to do so. When you didn't, I helped you."

"You… you…" Lord Northbridge sputtered. "I will speak to Burton about this, and you will be forced to leave the party. Not only that, but I will ensure you will never be welcomed at another event. I—"

"I would suggest that you rethink that, Northbridge."

They all turned in surprise at the new voice, finding Lord Andrew stepping out from an alcove across the room.

"What is that supposed to mean?" Northbridge had found his feet, catching the blood dripping out of his nose with a handkerchief from his pocket.

"I saw what was happening with Lady Noelle. She did ask you to leave her alone. I was about to step in myself when

Hartwell arrived. If you continue to make threats against them, I will have to share with the rest of the party why this all occurred."

"Why would you possibly side with this... with this..."

"I believe *man* is the term you are looking for," Cooper interjected helpfully, holding up a finger.

"Because Hartwell seems a good sort and you are in the wrong," Lord Andrew said with a shrug. "It's simple, really. Now, I would greatly appreciate it if you would all see fit to leave."

A giggle sounded from behind him, and a broad smile spread out on Lord Andrew's freckled face as he winked at them.

"Thank you, Lord Andrew," Cooper said, extending his hand to Noelle. "Shall we?"

She wore a muted smile as they left the room, Lord Northbridge moaning behind them, but they quickly distanced themselves from him. "I hope Lady Lucy has a good time with Lord Andrew," she said quietly.

"She seemed to be enjoying herself, although I'm not sure what her brother will think of it," Cooper said, a strange jealousy beginning to creep its way up his chest. Not that he was jealous of Lord Andrew, but he realized he was jealous that the couple was finding joy in one another, joy that he would love to find with Noelle.

But that wasn't an option. When they had made this arrangement, he hadn't realized just how much time they would be spending together, how close they would become as they were in this together, the only two who knew the secret.

"I've had enough dancing for one evening," she said suddenly, and he paused before they entered the ballroom again.

"What would you like to do?"

"Could we walk?"

"Outside?"

"If you don't mind."

"Not at all," he said, pleasantly surprised. "We'll need our cloaks."

He had to make sure she didn't catch a chill.

"I'll ask one of the servants," she said, reminding him of what different worlds they came from, that her first thought was to ask someone else to do it for her, while he would have gone to collect them himself.

Soon enough, they were dressed for the weather, which was milder this evening than it had been for the past couple of weeks.

"It has been cold lately," Noelle said as they stepped out the front door, him holding her arm steady to make sure she didn't slip on the frosty ground. "It is nice to take the chance to get some fresh air."

"Tell me if you get too cold."

"I will," she promised as they walked together around the gardens, which were, of course, decorated as the rest of the house was with ribbons, berries, and extra sprigs of evergreens among the hedgerows. A slight dusting of snow from the prior day had left a faint sprinkling of white over the leaves.

"It is beautiful," Noelle said wistfully as the half-moon rose in the sky, providing enough light to illuminate the path before them.

The path and Noelle's profile. When she spoke, Cooper turned to look at her and was taken aback by how beautiful she appeared that evening. He was always aware of her beauty, but she had an almost ethereal quality tonight. Rosiness had risen in her cheeks, her upturned nose pert, her lips as red as her cheeks. A sheen covered her eyes as she stared around them, and Cooper realized that this woman indeed took time to appreciate her surroundings.

She seemed comfortable in her soft, fine cloak, although it was worn in places that reminded him of the circumstances that had brought them together.

"How is your hand?" she asked.

It hurt like the devil, but he wouldn't tell her that. He guessed that Northbridge's nose hurt worse, and that was what truly mattered.

"Fine," he said with a shrug. "I apologize for that. I know that would have brought you embarrassment. I acted before I thought, which is uncommon for me. It will not happen again."

She looked up at him, their height difference quite evident.

"There is no need to apologize. If I am being honest, as much as I need to look after myself, I enjoyed having someone else look out for me for once."

"Does your father not do so?"

She lifted her shoulders up and down. "I love my father, and he is a kind man, but he is so absentminded that I am not sure he would even notice if anything untoward were to occur. He needs to be looked after, and I look after him, I suppose, more than the other way around." She shook her head as though to bring herself out of her musings. "What I am trying to say is thank you."

"You are most welcome," he said, unable to look away from her stare. She kept turning her glance from the path to him and back again as though looking at him was causing her to become disconcerted, which he understood. Every time her eyes met his, he was so mesmerized by her gaze that he wondered how he would ever allow her to walk away.

"We should be getting back," he said. "It's cooler out here than I thought."

"We should," she said, even though she remained exactly where she stood.

The space between them had lessened, though Cooper couldn't have said how they had moved together. She licked her top lip, and his gaze dropped, unable to move away from where that beautiful tongue had been. If only he could taste her lip for himself again. Even better still, her tongue.

He leaned in, ready to kiss her, but before he could press his lips to hers, she was gone, stumbling backward away from him.

"Cooper... I... we can't. Our contract. It's—"

"I know," he said gruffly, his hand rubbing the back of his neck. He had acted without thought. Again. A woman like Noelle wanted nothing to do with him. He might have money, but he didn't have a title, which carried much weight. Besides, even if she did, he could not promise her marriage and she was not the type of woman to give away affection without it. "I became carried away with the night air, the walk, the dance, and... everything."

"And everything," she repeated, before turning around and beginning to walk back to the house.

He couldn't stop himself from hurrying to catch her.

He couldn't keep himself away from her.

Which was going to become far too great a problem. For she was a young noblewoman, and he was nothing more than a businessman.

It didn't matter how much money he had.

She wasn't for him.

She never would be.

CHAPTER 10

*C*ooper hadn't said anything since he had caught up to her. Noelle was sure her cheeks were bright red, but it wasn't from the cold. Despite the weather, they were aflame with heat from Cooper. He had been seconds away from kissing her, and she had wanted it far too desperately.

It would have been so easy to have leaned in and met him halfway, but it would have been disastrous had she done so.

Disastrous for her.

For she remembered what it had been like to kiss him the first time. She had enjoyed it far too much and hadn't even known him then.

Now, she had spent enough time with him to know how thoughtful he could be. She knew how protective he could be. She knew how much she enjoyed his company.

It was becoming far too real, and while she was sure that to him, this was just a bit of fun, she was finding herself becoming more attached than she should have been. Having to continually remind herself that this was nothing more than a façade to further his business interests.

He might be a better man than she had initially thought, but he was still a businessman and fixated on getting ahead.

He was walking beside her silently, likely annoyed by her rejection of him, but Noelle knew she had just as much reason to learn more about this situation as anyone.

"Why does this all matter so much to you?" she demanded, turning to him abruptly with heated anger that he didn't deserve but was where her emotion found release. "Is this all just a bit of fun to you? You have done well enough for yourself already. Why do you need these people?"

She realized even as she said it that she wasn't including herself in the same category as the rest of the houseguests, even though she was just as much a part of them as anyone.

His nostrils flared slightly, but when he answered her, his tone was even.

"I have certain business interests for which I need parliamentary approval," he said. "If I had the right connections, I could get much further ahead than I could without them."

"These men are not going to talk politics with you."

"Perhaps not right away. I also need land. Land owned by people here or those that know them."

"What are these business interests of yours? What is so important?"

So important that he would use her like this.

"For credibility. And financial backing."

"There is more to it," she said, sensing the truth.

"That is nothing you need to concern yourself with. I can handle it."

"Why? Because I am a woman? Or because you do not trust me?"

"It is not that I do not trust you," he said, although his expression said otherwise. "It is just better to keep this to myself for now."

"Why?"

"Because if others were to learn what I am doing, they might use it to get ahead of me. I am certain I have competition. I just don't know with whom."

"Does this have anything to do with the investment my father lost?"

"This has nothing to do with Sanderson's investment," he said, but she still sensed that he was holding something back from her. However, it wasn't as though she could force it out of him.

"Well, perhaps one day you will learn to trust me," she said. "If you ever need to talk anything through, I can assure you that I know more of what I am talking about than most young women. My mother helped my father with many of his business interests and taught me how to do so."

She turned back toward the house, but he caught her forearms in his hands. His touch was firm yet gentle simultaneously, and she knew that if she asked him to release her, he would have done so without hesitation. But she didn't need him to.

"Noelle," he said, capturing her gaze. "I appreciate everything you have done for me and know you are trustworthy. It is just… my trust has been taken advantage of in the past, and it is difficult for me to share much with anyone else."

She nodded, still uncertain of where they stood with one another, but that would have to wait for another day.

"We are in sight of the ballroom," she said, gesturing toward the windows, although most were covered in so much frost that it would have been difficult for anyone to see out of them.

"Back in through the front doors, then," he said. "Remember, anytime this party becomes too much for you, I am more than happy to walk with you."

"Too much for me?" she repeated. "I should think I would be the one saying that to you."

"We all need some space now and again," he said. "Now, come, let's get you warmed up."

She wished he meant *he* would be the one to warm her up, but once they were indoors, he wished her goodnight and sent her off to bed with instructions to a servant to bring her warm milk.

It seemed he was not up to the task.

A pity.

* * *

COOPER HAD ALWAYS BEEN an early riser, which did not seem to be in unity with the rest of the house guests. He used the time for correspondence, as those in business with him knew where to send him letters. He had found a space in the library at a small writing table. It was much removed from the huge mahogany desk in his London home where he spent most of his time, but it would have to do.

He hadn't been lying when he told Noelle that his business interests were not the same as those in which her father had invested.

He just hadn't told the entire truth – that where Sanderson had failed, he had seen space to succeed. He just needed to move a few pieces into place before he could move forward, which a few of these men could provide.

Finished for the morning, he stood and stretched, ready to find the breakfast room and, most importantly, coffee. He was about to exit the library when voices from a room to his right filtered toward him.

"The tract of land between the canal and Lord Christopher's, yes?"

Why, how interesting. That was precisely the land he had been looking into acquiring.

"We still have his agreement, so long as the proper parameters are in place."

"The proper people, you mean."

"Yes."

Cooper inched closer to the door, needing to know who was speaking. Was he paranoid enough to believe that someone had perhaps killed the deal so that they could proceed without a few of the investors—namely him?

He was sure the others would say no. Yet he had a feeling, and his feelings were not usually wrong. That was how he had gotten to where he was today.

"It is most unfortunate that Hartwell is here."

Northbridge. Of course.

"He knows enough about the first deal that if he catches wind of this, he might put it all together."

Too late to avoid that now.

"Do we do the same with him as we did with Sanderson?"

"That might become too suspicious."

"Does it have to be?"

"I suppose not."

He needed to know who Northbridge was speaking with. It didn't sound like Lord John, but a couple of brief conversations were not enough to be certain.

"Send a letter to the same men as before. See if they can come out here."

"Is now the best time?"

"We must do this now before it's too late. Trust me on this."

"How much of this has to do with Hartwell, and how much the fact that you want his fiancée?"

"She is not my motive. She is the prize."

Cooper balled his hands into fists as red flashed across his vision. He took steps forward, no longer caring about what he would do, ready to slam the door open and tell them precisely what he was thinking when a hand reached out and caught his arm.

He turned around, his fist cocked, but he quickly dropped it when he saw who was there.

"Noelle," he whispered. "What are you doing?"

"Listening, as you are," she said, her arms crossed over her chest. "And if you go storming in there, you are not going to learn anything, but instead are going to put yourself in danger." She reached out, taking his hand and tugging him with her until they were in the shadows of the library across from the study. The study door was open just a crack, but Cooper could understand her thought – that if they waited here, they should be able to see when someone emerged.

She fixed him with a glare, one eyebrow raised as a tendril of her curly auburn hair bobbed down by her temple. She was dressed in a burgundy wool fabric dress, the high, lace-trimmed collar tempting him, but he would have to make do with running his fingers over the delicate white lace cuffs at the bottom of the fitted long sleeves. The small velvet buttons on her bodice were begging him to release them, but now was not exactly the time to concern himself with undressing her. Not when she was still staring at him with such annoyance.

"Now, will you tell me what is happening here, or do I have to ask Northbridge myself?"

He looked from one side to the other, seeking escape. This was far from ideal, but he supposed she was just as involved as he was. Steps sounded from down the corridor, and Cooper realized that they had no choice but to hide in the library, even if it meant they wouldn't see Northbridge's companions.

"Very well. Come with me."

He reached out a hand and led her deep into the library, near the corner writing desk. A pair of wingback chairs sat before it next to the frosty window, and he gestured for them each to take one.

"This does have to do with the railway," he admitted in a low voice.

"I knew it," she said, sitting up straight, fire in her eyes. "You lied to me."

"Not exactly," he argued. "It doesn't have to do with the same deal I was part of. I had new plans."

"Explain it to me, then," she challenged him.

"One of the reasons I invested in Sanderson's scheme was because I thought it was a good idea. That part of the country receives decent traffic and is not yet serviced by rail. When Sanderson disappeared, I was disappointed, yes, but I also considered that Cornwall still needed a railway, so why should I not continue it? I began to plan another venture. That is part of the reason I am here. I need a royal charter to expand and gain credibility in my dealings with the noblemen who own land that must be purchased to run the railway."

"Why do I sense a 'but' here?"

"It's what we just heard in that room," he said, his voice still calm. "The original deal is not as finished as I thought. I believe that Lord Northbridge and his conspirators in that room are not only continuing with the first deal, but they literally got rid of the people running it so they could move forward with their own."

She leaned in toward him, her eyes wide. "Do you think they *killed* Sanderson?"

He shrugged, leaning his chin on his fist. "Maybe. They were talking of bringing someone here from London. It could be whoever they used to eliminate the first men."

"That is a very severe accusation," she said.

He nodded, and Noelle rubbed her forehead.

"I am inclined to believe you," she said. "Men can do stupid things when it comes to money."

"I agree," he said. "Which is why this is so concerning."

"Do you honestly think they might try to get rid of you? Permanently?"

She said it so seriously that he would have chuckled at her dramatics if she wasn't so close to the truth.

"I have spent my entire life defending myself. It'll be just fine," he said, not wanting her to know just how lethal he could be.

"I am more concerned about you. Had I known these dealings would become so nefarious, I would never have involved you."

"Why would I be in any danger?"

"I am not certain that you are, but regardless, I need to keep you safe," he said. "If anything happened to you, I would never forgive myself."

"Why, Cooper, are you beginning to care for me?" she quirked a brow and one lip upward, but he shook his head at her blitheness about the whole thing, even though when he did so, her smile fell as though he was denying any feeling for her.

"Promise me that you will not go anywhere alone until we discover what is happening here?"

"Very well," she relented. "I promise."

"Good," he said, somewhat relieved now that she knew all there was to know. He hadn't liked keeping secrets from her. "Now, apparently, we are going ice skating."

"Of course we are." She laughed. "Have you ever skated before?"

"No."

"Well," she said, her smile growing, "you are in for a treat. Come, Cooper, let's teach you how to skate."

CHAPTER 11

$\mathcal{N}$oelle would never have admitted it to Cooper, but she was actually rather thrilled by all of this intrigue.

Not by the fact that anyone was in danger, but as much as Cooper seemed convinced that someone might be out to get him – them – she didn't think that any of the gentlemen here would have it in them to follow through with such an act.

It all seemed like something from a mystery novel, especially on a glorious day like today, with the sun shining down on them as they walked with their skates to the small lake on the estate grounds.

"Lord Bingly, Lady Lucy, have you met Mr. Hartwell?" she asked, catching up with the pair ahead of them. Lucy was Lord John's sister, while Lord Bingly was a young, quiet man who had only recently inherited his title. Like Lord Northbridge, he was a friend of Lord Leopold, Hattie's brother, who was away on the continent.

"Only at this party," Lord Bingly said in that quiet way of his. "How are you finding the festivities, Mr. Hartwell?"

"Enlightening," Cooper said with a steady grin. "And you?"

"This is not my first Christmas at Burton Manor, but it is the first without my parents," he said, a forlorn expression crossing his face. "It is not the same."

Noelle reached over and patted his hand. "I understand, Lord Bingly. It is, however, better than being completely alone at home in your manor that seems far too big for just you."

"That is true," he said with a forced smile as they crossed the small crest toward the lake. Wooden chairs had been set out on the shore next to the lake, which fortunately was shallow enough to have frozen this winter, as it had been frigid, even though the only snow to be seen was the odd dusting in pockets that didn't see much sun.

Noelle took a chair and bent over to untie her boot, surprised when Cooper knelt before her.

"Allow me," he murmured, and before she could protest, he lifted her right foot and placed it on his muscular thigh. His head was bent before her, covered in a blue knit cap, while he expertly untied the laces of her boot before reaching for the skate. He cupped her heel in his palm before slowly sliding it into the skate boot, her skin prickling even through her stocking where he touched her. His hands were large, warm, and strong as they guided her foot in, and Noelle closed her eyes for just a moment as she reveled in his touch.

"There we are," he said gruffly, and she opened her eyes to see that he had already finished tying it. "Is that too tight?"

"It's perfect," she said, and he nodded in satisfaction before he set her foot down and went to work on the other one. It was so easy, so natural, despite Noelle never having had such closeness with any other man.

When he finished her skates, he set her boots aside before

sitting beside her and working independently. With his skates tied, he stood on the grass, holding his arm toward her as they hobbled together to the ice.

Noelle held his arm for balance as she stepped onto the slippery surface first, but she soon let go once she found her footing, and years of skating came back to her. She even did a little twirl of glee as Cooper watched, still standing on the solid ground.

"Are you ready?" she said, holding her hands out to him. "I'll teach you."

"You'll teach me?" he said, lifting a brow as though questioning that she would have anything to impart.

"I am more competent than you might believe, Cooper," she said, placing her hands on her hips. He chuckled.

"I do not doubt that," he said. "Very well. Here goes nothing."

He reached out, took her hand, and stepped confidently onto the ice.

Then, he promptly fell straight on his behind, taking her down with him. She landed on top of him, and both of them let out an "oof."

Noelle pushed herself up on her arms, looking down at him with concern.

"Are you hurt?" she asked.

"I think it's just my pride," he groaned, and she couldn't help it. She started to laugh. At first, it was just a chuckle, but when he joined in with her, it turned into one of those full-body laughs she hadn't had in so long that she had nearly forgotten how. She could sense the stare of some of the other guests, but she had no care for what any of them thought. She only cared about herself and the man underneath her.

This was what had her suddenly realizing just exactly how he felt lying below her, her abdomen flush with his, her hips pressed against his until she felt a bulge below her that she knew was not just his hips.

Her cheeks flushed, and she scrambled off him, even as a shot of desire warmed her core most deliciously.

"I'm so sorry," she said, trying to stand but, in her hastiness, falling backward herself.

"Nothing to be sorry for," he said, his joviality fleeting as well as he had – quite clearly – felt some of the same longings she had. "This seems to be a bit trickier than I originally thought."

"It does take some getting used to," she said, finally finding her feet, holding out her gloved hands to try to help him, but he waved them away.

"I think I best try this once more on my own," he said, and she nodded in agreement.

"Very well."

When he finally rose, he pushed forward on the blades much more cautiously. He wobbled but found his balance before trying the other side. It was back and forth for a few more steps while Noelle waited until finally pushing forward beside him.

"That's it!" she encouraged. "You are doing it."

He wore a boyish grin as he slowly improved, step by step, and Noelle was surprised with her pride in his progress. She had been so focused on Cooper that she hadn't paid any attention to the rest of the group, who mainly had paired up and were skating in circles around the small pond.

"This isn't so bad, now, is it?" she smiled, reaching for his hand. He hesitated before finally placing his palm against hers, her gloved hand flush against his bare one as they continued on their path forward.

Noelle looked over at him, their gazes locking on one another as they shared an intimate smile – and missed what was ahead of them until it was nearly too late.

"Look out!"

They turned, Noelle stopping in time, but Cooper ran straight into Lord Northbridge, who had skated right in front of them.

Cooper went back to the ice with a crash while Northbridge, smaller yet much more experienced on skates, stood smirking down at him.

"You have no business being out here if you cannot stay on your feet," he sneered, causing Noelle's anger to simmer. "You'll only cause harm to the rest of us."

"You tripped him on purpose," Noelle accused, pointing her finger at him, noting with satisfaction that his nose wasn't as straight as it had once been, and dried blood was still apparent below it.

"I did nothing of the sort," he said. "It's not my fault the man is floundering around without ability."

"Listen here, Northbridge," Cooper said, trying to get to his feet, but his lack of purchase on the ice caused his threat to lose most of its edge. "You were bested and humiliated last night. It can happen again."

"Are you threatening me?" Northbridge said, loud enough for others to hear. Most ignored them, but Lord Burton must have felt it was his duty to intervene and skated over to them.

"Is there a problem?" he asked, looking back and forth from one man to the other, but it was Noelle who stepped forward.

"Lord Northbridge wasn't looking where he was going," she said. "Unfortunately, it caused a collision."

Lord Burton bent down and offered his arm to Cooper, helping him up. "Not injured, are you?"

"Might have a few bruises, but that's about it," Cooper said, straightening his cloak and jacket.

"Good," he said, looking from one man to the other, some warning in his gaze. "This house party means a great deal to my wife. Let us remember the Christmas spirit in our dealings with one another. Do you hear me?"

"Of course, my lord," Cooper said while Northbridge muttered something to himself. Burton leaned in.

"Christmas spirit, Northbridge, hear me?"

"Yes," Lord Northbridge said, his clipped tones earning him a frown from Lord Burton.

Hattie and Lucy skated by then, apparently needing to see just what was causing such commotion.

"Is everything well, Father?" Hattie asked.

"It should be now," Lord Burton replied with one last look of warning at the men.

"Lucy and I were just saying that when we are finished, we would love some hot chocolate, perhaps in the pavilion. Do you think Mother would agree?"

"I am sure she would be most happy with such a plan," he said. "I shall send one of the footmen to arrange it."

He skated away with a sullen Lord Northbridge following, Cooper watching their easy glides with undisguised longing.

"You shall get there very soon, Cooper," Noelle said, trying to ease the tension. "Look how far you've come in just a few minutes! In no time, you will be besting us all."

"By next Christmas, I'm sure you will be the fastest," Hattie agreed with a broad smile, causing a twinge in Noelle's stomach. For Cooper wouldn't be here next Christmas. By then, he would have long moved on from her to the next woman, business deal, or whatever the future might hold for him. All she knew was that it didn't include her. Nothing past Epiphany.

"I am sure," he said in a low, polite voice before the four

of them began skating the loop together, this time much more aware of their surroundings. Cooper did improve, but the joy that had been present between the two of them at doing this together was gone, removed by Lord North-bridge's arrival as well as the reminder that this was only temporary, that skating would soon be part of the past and not the future.

Which was exactly what they both wanted – was it not?

"Are you ready for chocolate?" Noelle asked after a few more half-hearted loops of the pond.

"Ready," he agreed, and they silently removed their skates. Noelle tried to remove her own skates, but Cooper insisted on doing it for her once again, holding her feet almost reverently before he transferred them to her boots. Their connection and emotion were strong, yet they were twinged with melancholy that Noelle could not quite explain.

They walked toward the pavilion amid other guests, listening to the chatter around them. The wooden chairs that had been situated near the pond had been moved to the pavilion, except there weren't enough for all the guests.

"I'll stand," Cooper said, motioning toward the lone chair remaining for Noelle to take, but she shook her head as she could tell that he was in a fair bit of pain from their skate.

"I think you should take it."

"The two of you are soon to be married!" Lady Hermione exclaimed. "I'm sure you could sit on his knee."

"Oh, I shouldn't," Noelle said, looking around them, but Lady Hermione waved a hand toward the assembled group.

"It is just the younger set of our group as my father has returned to the house and the rest stayed inside to play cards. No one would mind, I am sure. What is the worst that could happen? The two of you would be forced to marry?"

She laughed lightly, and Noelle forced herself to chuckle along with her, as Hermione had no idea she was speaking the truth. It would be the worst that could happen, at least from Cooper's perspective, she was sure. As for her, well, the thought of being married to Cooper was not quite as horrid as she'd once thought.

Not horrid at all, for that matter.

But rather... altogether too tempting.

CHAPTER 12

"I made a shocking discovery today," Noelle said to Cooper as they sat in the drawing room before dinner. They had chosen a corner slightly away from the rest of the party, primarily so Cooper could nurse his injuries privately.

He hadn't even told Noelle how many bruises had started to form, particularly over his ass and elbows.

It was not a pretty sight – even for a man who was no stranger to pain. In fact, he had lived off of it for a time.

"And just what was that?" he asked, ready for her to tell him she had lost any form of attraction to him whatsoever after seeing his incompetency on skates.

But, of course, that would suggest that she had been attracted to him from the start, which was not what this impending marriage was based upon.

"You, Cooper, have a sweet tooth. A very hungry one."

He laughed at that, for truer words had never been spoken. He wasn't sure how many cups of chocolate he had drank nor how many pastries he had eaten, which had been sitting on the tray served with the chocolate.

"It was one of the better cups of chocolate that I have had the pleasure of drinking, I will say that," he admitted. "I didn't see you declining a second helping either."

"I did not," she said with a sigh. "I also have a propensity for sweets. Just imagine what our children would be like." She stopped suddenly, her jaw snapping shut as she placed a hand over her mouth. "I shouldn't have said that," she said, shaking her head. "I only meant—"

"I know," he said, waving away her words. "It's fine."

It was fine. And yet, actually considering a future with her was fine as well. It was quite the conundrum, this fake engagement of theirs, which had become less of a business contract and more like an actual betrothal every day they spent together.

That was why she had included that clause of hers in the contract.

She was proving to be as smart as he was and likely should have been in charge of her family's business interests instead of her father.

She was quiet, then, her gaze on the wall of books behind him and her fingers moving against one another in a gesture that was becoming familiar. After watching her stitch the heart ornaments together, he guessed that her hands were usually occupied with a needle and thread, although she couldn't precisely carry them around here at the house party.

"A shilling for your thoughts," he teased, nudging her shoe with the toe of his boot. That caused a smile to glimmer momentarily on her face, even if it was rather sad.

"I'm afraid my thoughts are not worth nearly that much," she said forlornly.

"I disagree, and I am known to be a successful business-man," he said, reaching into his pocket and finding a coin before flipping it toward her. "Here you are. Now, a deal is a deal."

"I never agreed to this one."

"Humor me."

"Very well," she said shyly. "I was just thinking of my mother. What would she say about this entire situation? What would she want to do here at this house party? And, mostly, I'm just thinking about how much I miss her."

"I can understand that," he said, reaching out and covering her knee with his hand, noting how it fit completely overtop of it. One benefit of their arrangement was that a bit of chaste touch would not be questioned – it was even expected. "I wish I could bring her back for you, but that is beyond my ability. Is there anything that would make you feel closer to her?"

"There is a song she loved that I sometimes play," Noelle said shyly. "But I am not particularly adept on the piano."

"But you can play?"

"Yes, of course."

"Why don't you play now?" he gestured across the room where the pianoforte sat, but she was already shaking her head.

"Oh, no, I couldn't. No one wants to listen to my playing. Others here are much more inclined."

"I am sure they would still love to hear you play."

"I agree," came Lord Walters' voice.

Neither of them had noticed Noelle's father joining them, but he took the chair next to the sofa now, his smile warm as he leaned in toward Noelle.

"You play beautifully, Noelle, and Lady Burton always loves music at her house parties."

Looking from one man to the other, she finally sighed and relented.

"Very well," she said, pushing away from the sofa and striding toward the pianoforte. She may have resisted at first, but Cooper loved that once this woman decided on something, she gave her everything to it.

Like their fake engagement.

She sat at the piano, her fingers hovering over the keys, before taking a visible breath and beginning to play.

Cooper recognized the song, one which was popular at Christmas, of course. Her fingers danced over the keys more slowly than the usual tempo of the tune, but she was accomplished enough that he could sit back and enjoy it. He watched her with hooded eyes, taken aback by just how tempting she was, the candlelight glinting off her auburn hair, her entire body moving with abandon.

He looked around the room and realized he was not the only one captivated. Most guests had stopped to watch and listen, while a few men had undisguised temptation written on their faces.

There was only one thing to be done about that.

He stood from his place, hobbling across the room toward her. Her face lifted when she saw him lean against the piano beside her, and he winked at her before opening his mouth and providing words to the notes she was playing.

They looked up and saw a star
Shining in the East beyond them far,
And to the earth it gave great light,
And so it continued both day and night.
Noel, Noel, Noel, Noel,
Born is the King of Israel!

Their gazes caught and held, and for the next verse, she gave him a quick nod before joining her voice with his. Her voice might not have been perfect, but it was warm and throaty and caused desire to radiate through his entire body. Their voices melded perfectly together, creating one of those moments that sent tingles down his spine at just how right and perfect the blending was.

As they sang the final chorus of "Noels," he knew what he was singing, but somehow, along the way, it had become an ode to her, a joyous rendition of her name over and over.

As he stared at her, he realized the truth of the matter. They hadn't known one another long or well, but any moment he wasn't with her, he was looking forward to the next time he would see her. He was inclined to share his thoughts with her, whereas usually, he kept nearly everything to himself – even to the point of only ever telling his brother what was necessary.

It could be because of this secret he and Noelle had together, but he'd had many business dealings with other people in the past, secret agreements and confidential information shared.

Nothing had ever been like this.

And he guessed nothing ever would be again.

* * *

WHEN THE LAST notes trailed from Noelle's fingers, she found herself frozen in place, caught by the intensity of Cooper's stare.

He had not struck her as a man who would have enjoyed singing in front of a group of people, yet he had done so unabashedly.

For her.

What could it possibly mean? When she stared up at him, his navy blue eyes seemed to stare right through her soul, reading her every thought and emotion.

She had forgotten everyone else was watching them until a slow clap resounded from across the room. She broke their gaze as they both looked to the source of the sound, finding Lord Rochester had started the clap, soon to be joined by

Lord Andrew. Within seconds, the rest of the guests were echoing the applause.

Her cheeks had flushed with heat when she stood, placing her hand in Cooper's outstretched one. Noelle didn't mind the attention, but between her piano playing and being caught in such an intimate moment with Cooper, even she was overwhelmed.

As he led her around the piano stool, Hattie gasped so loudly that a few people's heads turned toward her.

"The mistletoe!" she exclaimed, pointing above them. Noelle stopped, her body knowing what that meant before her mind could catch up.

"Oh, we shouldn't," Noelle said, waving her hand. She couldn't say that the idea of kissing Cooper caused her great chagrin, but she wasn't sure about kissing him in front of the guests.

It didn't seem like they would have much choice, however, as everyone began to cheer and chant their names, urging them closer to one another.

"Kiss! Kiss!" came a few calls, and Cooper met her stare, his lips turned up at the corners. He looked up at what was indeed mistletoe strung above them—mistletoe that she had forgotten to look for—and shrugged, ready to give in to the pressure around them.

He reached his arm forward, curling his fingers around her elbow, slowly drawing her toward him, giving her plenty of time to back away. He stepped closer to her, leaning in, his face just inches from hers.

"This all right?" he asked softly, and she nodded.

Perhaps he would prefer not to kiss in front of everyone. But after this, no one could argue their connection. She lifted her face to his, closing her eyes as he softly pressed his lips against hers.

She knew that the kiss wouldn't go far. Not here, not with

everyone looking on. But no one else knew how all of her soul seemed to be melting into him, floating through the air along with their kiss where their lips were joined.

Her lips slightly parted, and if they were alone, she knew she would have welcomed him in and deepened this to a point that would have been difficult to break away from.

He was backing away from her sooner than she would have liked, and the moment his lips left hers, she already missed him, wishing there had been more.

More that could be hers in the future if she was willing to revise their contract and allow for physical affection.

But that would only bring them closer together, and closer was the last thing they should be – for it would only hurt all the more when he left her after this time together once he had received everything he needed from her.

He led her through the applause to a seat in the corner. It wasn't until they sat down that Noelle realized just how hard she was clutching his arm, and she hated that she was literally leaning on him to help her through a trivial occasion.

She had to be used to depending on herself, not on him.

She would have to resign herself to the fact that after this time with him she would have to marry whoever was willing to have her. At this point, her prospects would be low, but maybe with his contributions to paying off her father's debts, her father would at least be able to afford a small dowry. Perhaps she would have to find a vicar or someone similar who had enough respectability to see to her needs.

Noelle would rather be alone at this point, but she had enough wherewithal to realize she had no way to support herself unless she became a seamstress, the only skill with which she had proficiency. But even that would come with its difficulties.

As the thoughts ran through her mind, she knew she was only distracting herself from the truth.

That it wasn't her station in life that would be the saddest part of all of this.

It was that she would lose Cooper.

She had always loved Christmas and was saddened when it was over and the cold winter set in.

This year was no different – but it would only be all the worse when she had to say goodbye to the one man who truly saw her.

In the meantime, she would have to choose between distancing herself from him so that it hurt less when this was over or live in the moment and make the most of all the time they had together.

She looked over at him, catching his eye as he stared at her as though reading her mind.

He reached down, placing a warm hand on her leg.

And she desperately wished that he would never let go.

CHAPTER 13

*W*hen Cooper fell asleep that night, he was wrapped in a warm glow as he basked in his time with Noelle. Knowing that he had comforted and helped her in a moment of need meant more than he would have thought possible – especially to a man who, until this moment, would have considered this matter so trivial.

In the moments when they were together – whether it was singing as one voice or falling on his ass while skating or kissing her under the mistletoe – he forgot that this was a temporary arrangement, that *they* had an end date.

Part of him was wondering whether he still *wanted* this to end.

Was it possible that they could continue this past Christmastide? He had been confident in his bachelor status for so long, not interested in being tied down to anyone, and yet the more time he spent with her, the more he was tempted to reconsider his intentions.

He wasn't entirely sure whether she felt the same, but when she looked at him, the warm desire in her eyes had matched his own.

He might have fallen asleep with a smile, but he woke suddenly in the middle of the night, sitting upright in bed, confused.

He swiveled his head from one side of the dark room to the other, wondering what had woken him, when he heard another pop outside his window. He jumped from his bed, running to the noise.

He threw open the sash window, allowing in the frigid night air, but as he leaned out to see what was below, he could hardly make out anything in the dim light of the moon, which had increased ever so slightly since the night he and Noelle had walked together.

"Is anyone there?" he called out, and he heard shuffling below before footsteps running away.

That had been a gunshot. He was sure of it. He'd heard enough in his time.

He threw on his wrapper and grabbed his gun before opening the door of his room, relief flooding through him when the door across the hall opened at the same time and Noelle stood there, her own wrapper clutched around her, her unbound hair falling in curly waves around her face, nearly making him forget the situation at hand.

"What's happening?" she asked, eyes wide. "I heard what sounded like… well, a shot. Could that be possible?"

"I think so," he said grimly. "There was action outside my window. I am going out to check."

"You can't," she said, shaking her head. "What if someone is still out there with a weapon? You could be in danger."

He reached into the side of his wrapper, pulling out the pistol.

"I'm prepared," he said grimly. He had grown up in neighborhoods where he'd had no choice but to defend himself when the situation arose. He wasn't afraid of a nobleman who had fancied himself a brigadier for the night. "Stay in your room and lock the door."

"I should come with you."

"Absolutely not," he said. "If you come, I will be too worried about keeping you safe."

"Very well," she agreed, reminding him of her common sense. "But please come see me when you return."

"Worried about me, are you?" he said with a wink before hurrying through the corridor, down the grand entry staircase, and out the front door.

He shivered when he stepped out into the cold night air, orienting himself to the direction of his bedroom window and where the shot had come from.

He hurried along the ground floor, wondering if anyone else had heard the commotion, when he heard the front door open behind him and a shout ring out.

"You there – stop!"

He turned, lifting his hands. "I came to investigate myself," he called out, continuing on, not wanting to be slowed down by whichever staff or house guests had followed as well.

Cooper peered into the darkness. He was so focused on searching out anyone hiding in the shadows as a potential threat that he wasn't looking in front of him, and suddenly, he was stumbling, falling over a mound on the ground.

"What the..." he mumbled as he turned over just as more men approached, one of them holding a lantern out before him.

He cursed when he saw what – or rather, *who* – he had fallen over.

A very bloody, very motionless Lord Northbridge.

* * *

NOELLE KNEW Cooper needed her to stay upstairs, safe, but she was going crazy with worry, waiting alone, not knowing what was happening. She peeked her head out into the corridor as she heard multiple footsteps running outside and shouts from somewhere beyond the window and the house itself.

Realizing the commotion was coming from the opposite side of the wing, she slipped into the corridor and pushed open the door of Cooper's bedroom. The rush of cold air sweeping through it told her that his window was still open. She hurried toward it, peeking out to see a group of men below, approaching with a lantern casting light through the darkness.

Light on Cooper, who was sprawled on the ground – next to the motionless figure of what appeared to be Lord Northbridge.

Her breath caught in her throat when she saw that both men were covered in blood, and she put the facts together to realize that Lord Northbridge must have been shot.

And now Cooper had been found with him.

"Hartwell!"Lord Burton was leading the charge. "What have you done?"

"Absolutely nothing," Cooper said confidently as he rose. "I came out to investigate, just as you did. The shot sounded right below my window."

He pointed upward, and Noelle scrambled back, although she could have sworn that she saw Cooper's look of recognition as he caught her stare.

"I came out and stumbled right over top of him."

Lord Burton looked him up and down. "You are covered in blood."

"Yes," Cooper said with more patience than Noelle would have had. "Because I *fell* on him. It was too dark to see without a lantern.

"Is he dead?"

"Appears to be."

"There's nothing to be done now but to call the coroner."

That sounded like Lord John.

"True," Lord Burton said with a sigh. "I will send one of the footmen." He groaned aloud. "Lady Burton is not going to be happy about this."

Noelle snorted to herself. Lord Burton was so scared of his wife that it would have been humorous in different circumstances.

At least she could tell the coroner or whoever came to investigate that she knew Cooper was in his bedroom – that she had seen him open the door. She supposed it could be said that he would have had time to return to his bedroom after the shot, but she would bet her life that he had nothing to do with this.

Even if the victim *was* Lord Northbridge.

It seemed the entire house party was gathering outside. It had initially just been gentlemen, but when Noelle heard a scream pierce the night air, she knew it had to be Lady Burton, horrified that someone had dared to ruin her Christmastide house party.

It seemed an appropriate time to join the group below. Another Christmas gathering – this time a much grimmer one.

"Noelle, what is happening?"

Noelle emerged from Cooper's bedroom, hurrying down the corridor until she reached the stairs, where Hattie and Hermione were standing at the top. Lucy, her mother, and Lady Brighton and her mother were hurrying out from their bedrooms on the manor's opposite wing.

"It seems there has been an… incident," Noelle said hesitantly, not sure that she should be the one to break the news to the ladies. Hattie had shown some interest in Lord Northbridge, although she hadn't been as eager lately. However, it could still mean a change for her future, and it was shocking to have it occur in the same house where one was sleeping.

Then there was Hermione, who Noelle suspected had relations of her own with the man.

Hattie frowned, but after hearing another scream from her mother, she rushed out of the house, Noelle following. The ladies emerged into the night just in time to see Lady Burton faint into her husband's arms.

"Oh, Mother!" Hattie cried. "Father, what has happened?"

"I think we should convene in the drawing room," he said to the guests, who were now gathered together at the bottom of the stairs, most of them shivering from the cold, their breath visible in the air. "Hattie, call Mrs. Smith and have her take your mother to her bedroom. She is overwhelmed."

"But what—"

"I will tell everyone all that has occurred shortly."

Noelle listened to their conversation half-heartedly as she pushed through the guests, driven by her need to reach Cooper. When she caught sight of him through the window, she was taken aback by his expression. For a man usually so self-assured, he looked... concerned. She had a feeling she knew exactly why.

To be found covered in blood next to the very man he had met in an altercation the previous night? It was not a good look.

"Cooper!" she called out, nearing him, and he lifted his face, his eyes meeting hers – only his were filled with grief and desperation that she couldn't quite place.

"Stay back, Noelle," he said, but still, she pushed forward until a hand wrapped around her arm, and she turned to find her father holding onto her.

"He's right, Noelle," he said grimly. "You have to keep your distance."

"I will not," she said, her lips fusing together as she prevented herself from snapping out in annoyance as everyone tried to tell her what to do. "Cooper, are you all right?"

Before he could answer, Lord Burton's voice echoed throughout the night.

"One of the footmen has left to try to find the constable. He should be here soon enough, and in the meantime, we will wait in the foyer."

They were all primarily silent besides the odd murmurings between those close to one another as they filtered inside and waited — which luckily wasn't that long until Lord Burton announced the constable was coming up the drive. They all hurried outside to meet him.

A tall, broad-shouldered man strode up the side of the building, his steps as efficient as he must have been at his job.

"Everyone inside," he instructed. "Leave the lantern. The coroner and physician will arrive tomorrow. In the meantime, I will take down everyone's names and will examine the body, then guard it through the night."

Noelle stepped backward but didn't follow the rest of the guests inside yet. She had to wait and see what might happen to Cooper.

"Were you with him when he died?" the constable asked as he held the lantern up to inspect his clothing.

"No," Cooper said, his voice unwavering. "I heard the shot from my window and immediately ran outside to assess what was happening. In haste, I forgot a lantern and stumbled over the body."

"Very well," the constable said. "Well, it is not for me to do the questioning. That will come later. The coroner will have much more to ask you tomorrow, so don't go anywhere."

Cooper began walking toward Noelle, although both slowed when they saw Lord Burton leaning over the constable conspiratorially.

"As I am sure you are aware, Constable, we are in the middle of a Christmas house party, and this discovery has been distressing for my wife. I would appreciate it if we could keep this quiet. Do you understand? Perhaps this was a hunting accident?"

The man stopped examining the body, lifting the lantern to Lord Burton's face.

"Are you asking us to pretend this never happened? The murder could not be much more obvious."

"Of course not!" Lord Burton exclaimed. "Simply to use discretion in this death. We do not need everyone in England to hear about this, or we will never host another party. Our reputation will be ruined."

"As sorry as I am to hear of your potential loss of hosting duties, m'lord, it is not up to me. You'll have to take that up with the coroner, too. I'm only here to make sure no one touches the body. If you could send out a sheet of linen, I'll cover 'im for the night to preserve his dignity."

"Very well," Lord Burton finally relented as Cooper urged Noelle inside with a hand on her back.

All eyes were on them as they joined the rest of the guests in the drawing room. Suddenly, the festive greenery and mistletoe appeared out of place, as if it were a scene from another set – or, at least, another time.

"Mr. Hartwell, are you injured?" Noelle's father asked kindly, and Cooper shook his head.

"No. This is all from Lord Northbridge, I'm afraid."

"Lord Northbridge?" Lady Jennifer jumped up from her place on the sofa, her face pale. It was so odd to see all the guests, usually so properly dressed and covered in their finest, clothed only in their nightclothes and wrappers. "What has happened?"

Lord Burton shot Cooper a look, telling him he didn't appreciate him interjecting with the news. Lord Burton adjusted his features into their usual smoothness before he explained.

"Lord Northbridge is, unfortunately, no longer with us. From what we can tell, he was shot."

"Shot!" Voices rang out around the room as everyone began talking at once, the violence of his death just as shocking as the fact it had occurred. Lucy placed her arm around Jennifer and lowered her back down to the sofa.

It was Lord John's voice, however, that was loudest as he yelled out accusingly.

"That's why Hartwell is covered in blood – it was you! You shot him!"

The eyes turned back their way. Cooper said nothing, although Noelle could feel his chest rise and fall slowly, as though he was taking a deep breath to calm himself before answering the accusations. What was he to do? He could deny them, yes, but that wouldn't mean anything to these men.

Noelle's jaw clenched, every fiber of her being on edge, knowing what she had to do.

Cooper had no part in this. He had been in the wrong place at the wrong time and had only been trying to help. Instead, he was going to become a very convenient scapegoat. Not only was he already unwanted here, but there were also business dealings that the other gentlemen were trying to push him away from, and it seemed that he had ruffled some feathers by being engaged to her.

She was the only one who could save him.

"Mr. Hartwell had nothing to do with Lord Northbridge's

death," she said, stepping forward, her voice ringing loudly and clearly, everyone else returning to silence at her words.

"How would you know?" Lord John called out, his expression accusatory and disbelieving.

"Because," she said, lifting her chin. "I was with him when it happened."

CHAPTER 14

*E*veryone in the room stared at Cooper and Noelle silently – but no one was more shocked than Cooper himself.

He barely even realized that Noelle had slid her hand into his, holding on tightly as she stood bravely before them.

"Noelle," he murmured in a low voice. "Don't do this."

She looked up at him, her eyes unquestioning as she whispered, "Trust me."

Lady Brighton practically slid off the couch, her lips curling into a smile as she stared at the two of them. "Noelle, darling, are you saying you were in Mr. Hartwell's bedroom?"

"I was."

"I know you are betrothed, but that is rather... scandalous, is it not? You are not yet married."

"I am aware, Brighton, *darling*, but Mr. Hartwell and I are so in love we have a hard time not spending every moment together. This should be a private matter, but these circumstances give me no choice but to share the truth."

"I see," Lady Brighton said as Cooper couldn't decide

whether to be relieved or panicked. On the one hand, this meant that he would be saved from a murder accusation. But on the other…, he would now be forced to marry Noelle. How could he not? He knew enough about the nobility to be aware that, otherwise, she would be so scandalized that no one would ever consider marriage to her in the future. A broken engagement was one thing, but a broken engagement after admitting to being alone in the man's bedroom? There was no recovery from that.

It was true that he had been considering extending their relationship beyond Christmastide, but marriage was something else altogether.

She squeezed his hand as though sensing his unease, and he remembered what she had said. To trust her. It was not like he could do anything else at the moment.

"That is a romantic sentiment," Hattie said softly while Lord Walters looked back and forth from Cooper to his daughter in dismay.

"Well," Lord Burton said, his hands beneath his rotund stomach, "this has been a trying evening for everyone, and I am concerned about my wife. Why do we all not get as much sleep as possible and reconvene when the coroner arrives in the morning? We have a week until Christmas, and I hope we can finish this horrid affair before then."

The party all began to break up, the guests casting a mixture of suspicious and curious glares his way. Cooper, never one to shy away from attention, had never been more aware of it than he was in this moment.

He placed his hand on the small of Noelle's back again, enjoying the slight gesture of possessiveness that momentarily quelled his need to be close to her.

As they passed footmen, who appeared to have hastily dressed upon the commotion, he leaned into one of them.

"Could you please send up a small bath to my bedroom? I

apologize for the lateness, but..." he waved his hand over himself, and the footman nodded.

"Of course, sir."

"Father, could we have a word?" Noelle said as Lord Walters approached with Lord Aster, and he wearily nodded and excused himself as Cooper led the three of them into the small parlor at the back. Cooper wondered whether she was going to share the truth of their betrothal. It seemed the contract meant nothing anymore anyway.

Lord Walters began to talk the moment they stepped through the door, not allowing either of them a chance to explain.

"Mr. Hartwell, when I agreed for you to marry my daughter, it was with the understanding that you would care for her and protect her. Instead, you not only were caught with a dead body, but you have now compromised her and ruined her reputation. I—"

"Father." Noelle finally stopped him by stepping forward and placing both hands firmly on his chest. "None of this was Cooper's fault."

"Noelle," Cooper said, shaking his head. He was not about to let her take the blame for this. "That is not true."

"It is," she insisted, standing between the two men before lowering her voice after glancing at the closed door. "Father, this must stay between us, but I was not truly in Cooper's bedroom. I was in my own, but we both heard the gunshots. When I opened my door, he opened his simultaneously, with no blood stains on his wrapper. I realized, however, that if that was the story I told, a case could still be made that he shot through the window to create the noise or that I was lying for him. I had to be with him to clear his name. It's the only way."

"But your reputation—"

"I know it might come into question, but that makes my

story believable. Besides, I am not overly concerned," she said, her calm conciseness impressing Cooper. "Lord Burton wants to keep this entire situation quiet. I am sure that he will not be spreading news of what happened, and therefore, my reputation should remain intact from most of the *ton.*"

"And once you are married, no one will remember," Lord Walters added, causing Noelle's smile to falter for the first time since she had started on this.

"Yes," she forced out. "Of course."

"Well, there is nothing to be done about it now," Lord Walters said, running his hand through his short gray hair, causing it all to stand on end. "I am glad you did not compromise my daughter, Mr. Hartwell. I might have had some initial misgivings, but you have been a blessing to our family."

Or his money was. Cooper tried not to cringe at Lord Walters' sentiments, which seemed heartfelt. But knowing what they had agreed to, it was hard to ignore the guilt. He and Noelle needed to have a serious conversation alone.

Sooner better than later.

* * *

When Noelle returned to her room, she fell into bed, the plush blankets and pillows providing a cocoon of comfort. Despite her exhaustion, however, sleep remained elusive.

Every time she closed her eyes, all she could see was Cooper standing there, his gold wrapper bloody, and her heart jumped in her chest at the thought that it could have been him who was injured – or worse.

When she realized he could very likely be blamed for this, she had done the only thing possible.

She was aware of the repercussions and knew he was likely under the impression that he now had to marry her after her proclamation. But she would hold no man to her under false pretenses.

It was time to tell him so, or she was sure she would never find sleep.

She also needed to see him with her own eyes to ensure he was safe and to replace the image of him in his blood-soaked wrapper.

Finding her wrapper again, she opened the door as quietly as possible before tiptoeing across the hall and softly knocking on Cooper's door.

When she placed her ear on the wood, she could hear him rustling around within, and she took a breath, wondering what he would have to say to her after all that had occurred tonight.

"Noelle." He opened the door a crack before widening it and waving her in. "What are you doing in here?"

A bathtub sat in the corner of the room. It wasn't full but contained enough water for him to wash off. Water that was now tinged red. He wore only a pair of untied trousers that he must have hastily pulled on when she knocked.

"I'm so sorry. I've interrupted your bath," she said, stepping backward toward the door, but he reached out and caught her arm, holding her there.

"You didn't. I've finished," he said. "Are you well?"

"Yes, of course. I just… couldn't sleep."

She walked across the room and sat on the edge of his bed, crossing her arms over her chest.

"Are you cold?"

"I am, suddenly, yes."

"Go under the blanket," he said, jutting his chin forward, and she hesitated despite how enticing his bed appeared.

"It will be our secret." He winked. "Although I don't suppose discretion matters much anymore."

He was right. She nodded in agreement before nestling

under the blankets, which smelled like pine needles and leather. Like him. She hoped he didn't notice how deeply she inhaled, taking him in.

As much as she wished for the man himself, he kept his distance, sitting on the opposite corner of the bed. "Now, tell me what you need."

She wanted a lot from him, but that wasn't what he had asked.

"I need to tell you that I have no additional expectations from you," she said. "Our agreement remains the same. I know that my lie might change things for you. The gentlemen won't like the idea of you compromising me, but it would be far worse if they believed that you were a killer. I couldn't let them suspect you for Lord Northbridge's murder and could see no other way around it."

He leaned over to lie on his stomach, facing her.

"Noelle, if you stick to this story, *you* will be ruined if we do not marry. I was looking forward to the support of some of the gentlemen in attendance at this house party, but I can still find my way forward even if I lose it. What will you do if you do not marry? Who will support you?"

"My father will while he is able, and then, well, I may have to marry down, but I do not need finery. However, I do not believe that this will cause my ruination. I meant when I said that this will likely be kept quiet. You heard Lord Burton. He is trying to prevent this from even being labeled a murder. I can see them avoiding an inquest altogether."

"We will see what the coroner says tomorrow. But you don't have to stick to this story. I didn't murder Lord Northbridge, and I am sure that all will be revealed in due time. Just tell the truth – that you saw me leave my room moments after you heard the shot."

"It will not be enough. It would be easy for me to lie about that. It is not so easy for me to say that I was here with you, knowing what is at stake."

Cooper pushed himself up from his prone position, striding off the bed and pacing back and forth, his face pinched in concentration. Noelle's heart beat in time with his footsteps, but she remained silent, her eyes even closing momentarily as she allowed him to work through whatever he was thinking. Finally, he seemed to have reached a conclusion, for he stopped, braced his feet wide, and looked at her.

"We must marry in truth."

Her jaw dropped. That was the last thing she expected of all the things he could have said.

"We cannot!"

"Why not?"

"Because... because you do not want a wife."

"Perhaps not," he agreed. "But what are you going to do now? You cannot be certain that you will ever be able to find another man to marry you – at least one that can keep you in the comfort you are used to."

She bristled at that. "I am not so fine that I—"

"I know." He held up his hands. "That is not exactly what I meant. Hear me out. It will be difficult to find a man who can provide you all you deserve and support you so you will not have to work yourself – especially without a dowry. The reason that I do not want to marry is that I do not want to be tied down or beholden to anyone. Perhaps we could come to another agreement that will benefit both of us."

"Another business contract?"

"Something like that," he said, walking over to sit down next to her. She pressed her back against the headboard as he placed one of his large hands over both of her smaller ones, and he looked earnestly into her eyes.

"We could marry but agree that we can each live our own

lives. I will be free to continue my business dealings and not feel any obligations to my life at home, and you will feel supported financially and able to live your life as you will. See who you want. Attend any social engagements. Look after your father. Do as you wish with the house. Sew for your own enjoyment. I also think you could help me."

"How?" she asked, shocked at everything he was proposing.

"You have a fine mind. There are certain aspects of business in which you could help me. As my wife, I am sure you would be available to help me undertake certain dealings that are easier for a married man than a single one. For example, dining with another couple if I must do business with the man. You would be an excellent hostess. Not only are you polite, but you also understand business matters."

"I see," she said, biting her lip. She had always hoped that she would love the man she married. But perhaps it would be much more realistic to *like* her husband. She respected Cooper and could admit that her body was more than open to marriage with him.

There was one question on her mind, though. One that shouldn't matter. Not if this was a business dealing as opposed to the romantic proposal she had always hoped for. But suddenly, it held more importance than she would like.

"Would you, ah… take other women to bed?" she asked softly, unable to meet his eyes. "I know it should mean nothing to me, but I would just want to know so that I was never asked and taken aback. It would not do us any good for that to be known, not when the entire premise of our being together was romantic."

He ran his hand over the side of her face before cupping her cheek, stroking it with his thumb. She leaned into it, hating how much she loved his touch.

"I would never do that to you," he said softly, although he

didn't clarify whether he would never find another or be discreet. "Now, you are tired. Go to sleep. We will figure this out tomorrow."

"Cooper?"

"Yes?"

"Could you... could you hold me? I'm cold and tired, and I just..."

She couldn't say the rest. That she wanted him to look after her. That she was more comfortable here than alone. That it made her feel better to have him with her than picture him murdered in her nightmares.

Somehow, he seemed to understand anyway.

"Of course," he said, sliding into the bed behind her. He reached his arm around her, tucking her close into his body, his hard chest flush against her back.

"Goodnight, Noelle."

"Goodnight, Cooper," she said, relaxing into him.

Within moments, she fell fast asleep.

CHAPTER 15

*C*ooper didn't sleep a wink, yet he had never woken more content.

Even with a murder accusation hanging over his head and soreness through his entire body, from falling all over the frozen pond to tumbling over Lord Northbridge.

Noelle had slept soundly in his arms the rest of the night, oblivious to his own inability to sleep, what with his need to comfort her, his urge to protect her, and his raging need for her. Need that didn't appear to be going anywhere.

He was sure she would have been horrified if she had awoken to feel the evidence of his desire for her, though he kept his hips shifted back away from her. The feel of Noelle in his arms, in his bed, the soft cinnamon scent of her hair, the silk of her nightgown beneath his fingertips – it was all nearly too much. He hadn't even touched her intimately, and he had already been close to coming in the bed behind her.

But if this was what she needed, he would do it.

It was his job to keep her safe and happy.

He had promised her father.

And now her, in his request to become her husband.

He still hadn't fully grasped the ramifications of what he had proposed, but he had no time to think of that now – not when he could hear movement beyond his bedchamber door.

Cooper leaned down to wake Noelle, but seeing how soundly she was sleeping, he decided to try not to disturb her. He slid out of bed, silencing a groan at his protesting muscles, careful not to wake her, before opening his bedroom door a crack and peering out into the corridor. Whoever had walked by – likely a servant – seemed to have gone. He padded over to Noelle's door, opening it wide before returning to his room.

He leaned over his bed and gathered Noelle in his arms, loving how she snuggled into him, tucking her head under his chin as she let out the smallest snores.

He smiled as he crossed the hallway and laid her in her own bed, taking a moment to stand and watch her in sleep – as though he hadn't done enough of that already. She was so relaxed, so calm, so beautiful.

And now, she was his.

In a way.

He hated leaving her without him, wishing to be beside her when she woke.

But he supposed he would have plenty of time to do that once they were married.

This gave him an idea—one that might be rather inconvenient after what had occurred last night but might save their reputations and clear his name from any involvement in this murderous affair.

Cooper was a man who, once he made up his mind about something, preferred to take action quickly, before the impulse left him.

That was why he was nearly bouncing in impatience when he saw Noelle – an awake Noelle – later that morning.

Unfortunately, the rest of the guests were also in attendance, gathered around the breakfast table. It wasn't silent by any means, but everyone spoke in low murmurs, as though speaking aloud would wake the dead or cause the speaker to become a subject of suspicion.

Cooper sat next to Noelle, her father on her other side. Cooper leaned down and squeezed her hand, earning him a small smile.

"Thank you," she said quietly, lifting her cup of tea to plush, red lips. Lips that he would very much like to taste once more.

"For what?"

"For allowing me to stay with you last night. For providing me with the comfort I needed. I feel much more refreshed this morning."

"I'm glad of it. And I'm happy to do it. In fact, Noelle," he began, needing to tell her of his plan, but he was interrupted when Lord and Lady Burton entered the room. Lady Burton appeared rather pale and peaked but determined to continue this party.

"I apologize to everyone for what occurred last night," she said. "Lord Burton has promised me that we will quickly deal with this matter and then return to our festivities. In the meantime, we will continue to enjoy the food, décor, and all that can provide comfort in this trying time. As you can imagine, Lady Jennifer has declined to join us today."

"We have all been asked to remain at the estate," Lord Burton added, focusing on the guests in front of him, causing him not to notice the new presence in the room, a man who walked up and stood behind him.

The newcomer possessed an air of authority. He was much taller than Lord Burton, thin, and with a pinched face. His gaze wandered around the room, landing on each of them suspiciously.

Lord Burton finally noted the direction of the gazes of

the assembled breakfasters and turned around, starting when he realized they were no longer alone.

"I would like to introduce the coroner, Mr. Briggs," Lord Burton said, backing up a step. "He arrived this morning and has already examined the bod— Lord Northbridge. He would like to ask us all a few questions."

"That will not be necessary today," Mr. Briggs said, holding up a finger in the air. "We shall do that at the formal inquest, which will be held in Gulliver's Tavern."

A low murmur started up among the guests at that news until Lord Burton turned to him with a pained expression. "Mr. Briggs, I was under the impression that we would keep this... quiet."

"According to whom?"

"Well," Lord Burton drew himself up to his full height, although he still didn't come much higher than Mr. Briggs's nose. "Me. I am the lord of this area, and I would prefer that this didn't cause much gossip among the inhabitants and the *ton* beyond. We would happily cooperate in any way possible, but perhaps we could do so without a formal inquiry."

Mr. Briggs looked down his nose at him, sniffing as he obviously couldn't voice what he was honestly thinking. "There will be an inquiry one way or the other," he said. "But perhaps we could do it here instead of at the tavern. We would still need a jury to attend. They will determine just whether or not this is murder and the magistrate will decide whether we can determine a suspect. If so, the suspect will be tried at the assize – or the House of Lords – but not until after the holiday season."

Lord Burton did not seem particularly pleased, but he did seem to realize this was the best offer he would receive. Lady Burton, meanwhile, turned rather pale, and Hattie rose, urging her mother into a chair while fanning her face.

"Very well," Lord Burton sighed, waving a hand. "If that is what must be done."

"We will summon the jury for tomorrow."

"Tomorrow!"

"Yes. This must be dealt with quickly. You did say you wanted to take care of it before Christmas, did you not?"

"I did," Lord Burton sighed again. "I most certainly did. Very well."

He clasped his hands together and looked over the assembled group. Cooper noted the mistletoe mockingly hanging low over his head. "We will reconvene this afternoon as we will search for a yule log. Take the next few hours to do as you wish."

The guests stood, looking at one another in bewilderment. Lady Hattie's eyes were red as she sat across from Noelle, wringing a handkerchief between her hands.

"This is all so unbelievable," she said, speaking to Noelle as Cooper met the eyes of Lord Rochester behind her, who seemed ready to soothe her. "In my own home?"

"Hard to believe something like this could happen, especially at Christmas," Lord Rochester said as the branches of the Christmas tree behind him poked him in the shoulder as though to emphasize his words. "Who would have it out for Northbridge?"

As he said it, the air crackled with tension, Rochester realizing belatedly just what he had said and how that could be insinuated.

"I know the two of you weren't on best of terms, Hartwell, but it seems it wasn't you, now, was it?" Lord Rochester wore his usual grin, but it wasn't as friendly as before. Cooper realized that this was likely what to expect in the future. No one could outright accuse him of anything, but he was the outsider here. They would protect their own.

"It was not," Cooper said from behind his smile. "I may be ruthless in business, but I do not deal with violence."

"Of course not," Lord Rochester agreed with a disbelieving smile as Noelle and Hattie watched the exchange with wide eyes.

"Who do you think did it?" Lady Lucy asked, leaning forward as they all stared at each other suspiciously.

"I do not believe it was someone from this group," Lady Hattie said, shaking her head. "How could it be? None of us would ever do such a thing to Lord Northbridge. It could have been someone who traveled here to the estate. Or perhaps even a servant, although ours are all loyal to us."

"I'm sure the coroner or the magistrate will determine whether anyone traveled here yesterday," Cooper said, wishing to break up this conversation. "They would be able to check for tracks at the lake."

He was beginning to question just how competent the local authorities might be. They had spoken about solving this before Christmas for Lord Burton's sake, but Cooper felt that those investigating, to say nothing of the jury, would prefer to return to their own families for Christmas.

Perhaps he would have to take this matter into his own hands, or he just might receive a murder charge for Christmas.

"Noelle," he said, turning to her and ignoring the rest of the table. "Would you like to go for a walk?"

"It is cold today," she said before looking into his eyes and reading that he had hidden intention behind his question. "But yes, fresh air would be lovely."

They gathered their outdoor wear, although Noelle still shivered when they stepped out of doors. The sky was gray today, and while no snow had yet appeared, it was threatening.

"If it snows, do you suppose that anyone will be able to travel to the estate?" she asked, and Cooper shrugged, the thought not having occurred to him.

"I do not suppose that is much our concern, now, is it?"

Noelle stared at him, brows drawn together as though trying to assess what he meant by it when she noticed where they were.

"Cooper, why are we here?"

Here, being the site of the murder. The body had been removed, although an imprint in the ground remained, the dry brown grass indented where Lord Northbridge had lain.

"The area is not exactly preserved, what with the number of people who came outside last night," he murmured as he walked around, trying to find what he was looking for.

"You haven't answered me."

He looked up at her. "I have a feeling that this might not end well for me. You heard Lady Hattie. They cannot imagine anyone doing this. Anyone from their own circle. That leaves me."

"But I was with you. I will tell the jury that."

"I know. But to be on the safe side, I thought I might see what I could figure out myself."

He crouched low to the ground, searching through the grass, triumphantly pointing out the evidence.

"It's here."

"What is?"

"Look closely. Do you see the small pieces of metal on the ground?"

She crouched beside him, leaning on his thigh to help her balance.

"Yes, I do."

"After a percussion cap pistol is fired, the small copper or brass percussion cap that ignites the gunpowder ruptures. It can leave these little metal pieces behind. They can be cleaned up, but it would be difficult without time and in the dark."

"What does that mean?"

"It means that we know what kind of gun we are looking for," he said grimly. "I am assuming there is also a bullet inside of Lord Northbridge that could determine which gun was used."

Noelle grimaced. "That is gruesome."

Cooper suddenly felt a boor for discussing this in such detail with her. "I should apologize. You likely have no wish to speak of this, and here I am, going on about it—"

She placed a hand on his. "It's fine. I can handle it."

"Sometimes I forget that you are a lady, and this is not the kind of talk for a woman like you."

"Cooper. I am not your typical lady. That, I can promise you. If I can help you determine the truth, I am happy to do so."

"Very well. I do appreciate that. I will suggest to the coroner that he look for this later. We must determine if anyone has access to such a weapon." He took her arm, leading her away from the scene. "But that is not the only reason I wanted to have you alone."

"No?" she said, arching her brow.

All of the other things he would like to do with her alone ran through his mind. "Have you thought any more about getting married?"

"That is not exactly something that slips one's mind."

"This might seem hasty, but I have been thinking… maybe we should get married sooner rather than later."

She tilted her head, her nose, which had become rosy with the cold, crinkling deliciously as a curl fell out from her knit cap.

"How soon are you thinking?"

"Christmas Eve."

Her lips parted. Her eyes widened.

And then she laughed.

CHAPTER 16

$\mathcal{N}$oelle immediately regretted her laughter when the light in Cooper's eyes dimmed slightly.

He had been excited to bring this to her, she realized. She had just been so caught off guard that she had reacted without thinking.

"I am so sorry, Cooper, but Christmas Eve is in six days! That will not even be possible."

"I know it is quick and no, there will not be the usual reading of the banns, but Lord and Lady Burton are well known in this area and your father has connections as well. If we accompany them to appeal to the vicar, hopefully it should be enough to achieve Expediency on an Ordinary License. If we are allowed, I see no impediments."

"No, but…"

"But you do not want to be married to me."

When his face fell, she reached out and grabbed his forearms.

"Cooper. I agree with your suggestion that we marry, even though I am still concerned that you will regret this decision. It is just... soon. Although I must say, you have done your research on how to marry quickly."

"I was told the scenario while educating myself about the nobility and most facts stay with me. I thought that if we marry now, we will face less scandal, and our story of you in my bed would be more believable."

She stepped closer to him, drawn by the warmth in his body and the heat in his gaze.

"You think that we do not appear infatuated by one another?"

She inclined her head, gasping slightly at how close his face was to hers, how strong his jawline was, and how enticing his scent was.

This had started as a sham of an engagement, yes, but now she couldn't help but remember what it had felt like to be surrounded by his body last night. She had been exhausted and on edge then, appreciating his thoughtfulness, but now... now she saw him in a different light.

She wanted to be close to him, and not just for his protection or the comfort he provided. She wanted what he could offer her as a man. As a husband.

She wasn't sure if that should excite her or scare her.

He reached up, cupping her cheek, his palm rougher than most men she was acquainted with.

She liked it.

He stroked her cheek with his thumb, leaning in.

"I am becoming more enamored with you than I ever thought I would," he said gently, causing Noelle's pulse to quicken. "May I kiss you?"

"I suppose we *are* going to be married," she said, even as she knew that she was the one at risk of becoming enamored.

He was beginning to reveal that he was the type of man she could fall in love with.

But falling in love with a man who was only interested in a marriage of convenience could be the most significant risk, for she saw only one destination – a broken heart.

Even so, she could still have a little fun… could she not?

He leaned down slowly, giving her plenty of time to pull away if she chose.

She chose not to.

Instead, she lifted her face and closed the distance between them.

They had kissed before, yes, but the first time, they had been strangers, and the last time, they had been in front of a gathered crowd to appease those who wanted to see proof of their relationship and were interested in a bit of Christmas fun.

This kiss was for no one but one another, which made all of the difference.

The only other man Noelle had ever kissed was one she would rather forget at this moment – which Cooper made it easy to do.

His lips were firm against hers as she wrapped her hands around his neck and increased her own pressure. His leathery-pine scent intoxicated her, causing her to forget all reason.

For a man so intensely hard, his mouth was soft as he proved that he had as much expertise in this as he did in everything else. Noelle couldn't help but let out a moan when he plunged his tongue inside, a deep growl vibrating in his chest as his hands moved from her face to wrap around her waist and pull her up against him.

Last night, she had discovered just how hard and muscled he was.

Today was a reminder.

It was also a lesson that what Noelle had thought was a kiss in the past was not a proper kiss – not like this one. This was a true plundering, as he pressed her backward until she was standing against the house, the rough brick scratching the material of her jacket.

Cooper must have understood, for he slid his hands down beneath her bottom, taking a moment to greedily cup her before pulling her hips to his, and she nearly had to clench her legs together at the feel of him.

This was... not what she had ever expected. She knew some women desired their husbands while others put up with them.

This marriage might not be genuine in their feelings, but there was enough lust between them to make that part of it true.

He allowed no space between them, and their lips never separated or stopped moving. His kiss and his touch caused every inch of her skin to heat deliciously in contrast to the cold winter air.

Finally, he broke this kiss although he didn't pull away from her, instead moving his lips to her ear. His voice was soft and low as he murmured, "Tell me again that you do not want to be married."

"I—" She was at a loss for words.

"I most certainly do. I cannot wait until we are married. Have you ever considered there are more reasons I would like to do this quickly? Ever since we met, I have wanted you... thought about you. Last night, when you were in my bed, it was hard to keep my hands off you."

"Cooper," she groaned as she melted into him, clutching the edges of his cloak in her hands. If he wasn't holding her upright, she might have fallen to the ground at his feet.

"Our marriage will be beneficial to both of us, Noelle. I promised you that I would not take any women to bed. I meant any *other* women. Do you understand?"

"I – yes, I think I do."

He was going to take *her* to bed.

And she could hardly wait.

* * *

COOPER HAD ALLOWED his passions to get away from him.

He had practically ravished Noelle at a murder scene, and now here he was, back outdoors, traipsing around an estate looking for a damn yule log.

When Lady Burton gathered them all and began explaining the activity, it was evident she was trying to hold herself and this Christmas party together. Her face was drawn, her husband supporting her with an arm behind her back as they had all stood in cloaks near the entrance.

This murder and subsequent investigation, however, had also brought them all, rather strangely, together. Everyone at the house party but Lady Jennifer was present for this, even though the chilled air had already begun to freeze Cooper's toes, and he had a feeling that his boots were much thicker than those most of the others wore.

"We are looking for a large branch, hopefully one that is rather dry," Lady Burton said. "Why do we not all split into groups of four and look in various areas of the estate? We can each select a tree as an option, and then Lord Burton will look at all the candidates and determine which one we will have our groundskeeper cut down for our selection."

Groups of four so that no one else would be at risk of being murdered, Cooper thought wryly, although he didn't dare to voice it aloud.

That was one thing he had quickly learned when working with nobles – nearly every thought that mattered remained unspoken.

"Shall we?" he asked Noelle, holding his arm out, and she nodded, pressing herself close against his side as she had earlier. He guessed that she was stealing his warmth, although he would give it to her gladly anytime. He hoped she also enjoyed his closeness, but he didn't want to assume anything.

He was already becoming obsessed with her body. He couldn't allow himself to become even more infatuated, or he would be in great trouble.

He was open to marrying her, yes—he even *wanted* it now. But he had seen lesser men fall in love and forget everything else in their lives, losing at business practices when they could no longer focus their attention on what was necessary.

He would not be that man.

"I have not forgotten my promise to you," she said softly. "Is there anyone you need to spend time with?"

"Hartwell!"

It seemed they would not have a choice as Lord John strode purposefully toward them, his generous eyebrows lowered over his eyes. "Shall we go together?"

"Why not?" Cooper said with a forced smile, for he knew that Lord John must have additional motives for wanting to spend time with him besides his company.

"Lady Hermione, would you like to join us?" Noelle asked. Cooper was grateful she hadn't asked Hattie, for her red-rimmed eyes and quivering lip told him that she was distraught over Northbridge's death, even though the man had never seemed overly affectionate toward the girl.

"I would love to," Hermione said, practically bounding toward them. She was as energetic as her mother, although it appeared that Hattie had inherited the histrionics.

Cooper preferred this, even though they would receive an earful of chatter from what he had seen so far.

They better find this yule log fast.

They broke out into different sections of the estate, and Cooper shared a look with Noelle that she understood – one of the reasons he so appreciated her. She was to keep Hermione entertained while he and Lord John came to terms with whatever the man wanted from him.

"How is your family holding up?" Cooper heard Noelle ask, which was all that was required for Hermione to launch into a soliloquy that basically said her mother was trying to keep the house party together, her sister was distraught over her lack of prospects as she had been relying on Lord Northbridge, even though Hermione thought him a poor choice, and her father wanted to pretend that none of this had ever happened.

"Lord John," Cooper said as he kept his eye on the path – and the trees – in front of them, "shall we dispense with the chatter? Was there a reason you wanted to keep me company or was it simply for my charming manner?"

Lord John snorted. "There is no need for the coroner's inquiry. We both know that Northbridge was murdered."

"Doesn't seem to be many other explanations for a bullet hole through the chest at close range, now is there?"

"You're the only one of this group that doesn't fit. You know that?"

"I have been made aware," Cooper said wryly. "I realize how opportune it would be for all of you if I was the one who killed him. But, unfortunately for you, it was not me, as my lovely soon-to-be bride can attest to. I would, however, be happy to help you find the true killer. It would clear my name and allow me to leave this estate without any stain upon my reputation."

"You do know, Hartwell, that I will not allow that land to be yours."

Cooper lifted his brows and chin as he took measure of the man, whose gaze remained ahead.

"You'll have to elaborate."

"Do not pretend not to know what I am referring to. You

did away with Sanderson and are trying to build the railway yourself."

"I had nothing to do with Sanderson's disappearance. Why would I, when I had a great sum of my own money tied up in the thing? However, the need is still present. Why should I not be the man to provide it?"

"You are not the only one to feel this way."

"So I hear."

"I own some of the land that you would need, but I am not inclined to sell it to you."

"Do tell me, Lord John, why I am such an inconvenient choice for you."

"Because it was your fault that we all lost money in the first place."

"Ah," Cooper said, recognition finally dawning. "You were one of the investors who blamed me for the loss. Well, I am sorry to have to educate you on how investing works, but first, you should not invest money you do not have, for there is always the chance of losing it. Otherwise, it would not be an investment. Second, I lost money just as you did. Third, I did not convince anyone to invest. You all did that on your own."

"When *you* invest, it is a sure thing."

Cooper let out a bark of laughter, noting Noelle's attention.

"You chose to follow my lead all on your own. You must understand that everyone makes mistakes," Cooper said with a shrug. "I cannot be right every time, as much as I would like to be. That being said, why do you not come on board with me in this next venture? I can assure you that I would never lead an undertaking of this magnitude without certainty that it will all come to fruition."

"I have already been approached."

"By whom?"

"I cannot say."

It was whoever Northbridge had been speaking to in the study that night; Cooper was sure of it. But he couldn't say so now without revealing that he had been eavesdropping.

"I will leave the choice to you," Cooper said. "But I might have an offer you cannot refuse."

"I look forward to receiving it," Lord John said as Cooper wondered whether the man could be capable of murder himself. Had he and Northbridge disagreed over the deal? And how was Cooper supposed to convince the man to allow him the land he required now? Lord John owned a critical piece. To go around it would cost more than the railroad was likely worth. He would have to determine his rival in this railroad venture.

It didn't seem that Lord John was inclined to tell him.

"There!"

He turned at Noelle's voice to find her pointing excitedly along the path ahead. "Up there – could that not be used for the yule log?"

The tree was dying, its high branches dry and bare of any remaining leaves. If a few twigs were removed, it could make for a fine yule log.

At least, according to what Cooper had learned before they left the house. He had never actually seen a yule log before but had learned that it would need to burn through most of Christmastide. To have participated in such a custom before would have required a forest to be in front of him, which wasn't exactly at his family's disposal.

"That looks well enough to me," said Lord John, who had as much interest in this yule log as Cooper did.

This was why he had come here – to spend time and better come to know gentlemen such as Lord John. And now that he was here, he wanted to leave Lord John and his pompous opinions behind and spend time with Noelle instead.

"Lord John, would you like to return to the house together?" Noelle asked, causing Cooper's teeth to grind against each other. Why on earth would she not choose him for the return journey? Not only would he have to watch her with Lord John, but now this meant he would be subjected to Lady Hermione, the epitome of young ladies that he couldn't stand.

He sighed until he caught the curve of Noelle's smile and her wink. She had some idea in mind, although he couldn't imagine it. Maybe she thought she could work some magic with Lord John, although from what he could tell, the man was beyond any attempts to ingratiate himself.

He had it out for him, and Lord Northbridge's murder had only made matters all the worse.

He had to find who had done this – sooner rather than later, especially if he wanted to enjoy his wedded bliss with Noelle, which he fully intended to do.

In fact, he could hardly wait.

CHAPTER 17

*A*fter saying goodnight to Cooper and walking into her bedroom – alone – Noelle realized that he had a point. Perhaps six days wasn't too long at all. Maybe it was not soon enough.

She did want to share some thoughts with him after the day with the other guests, so after her maid finished preparing her for sleep, she opened her door to sneak into his bedroom—and nearly walked right into the man himself, waiting on the other side.

"Where are you going?" he asked with wide eyes.

"Where do you think?" she said with a bit of a laugh, opening her door wider. "Come on in."

He stepped through the door, his gaze wandering around the room, taking in the red drapes, the red and gold canopy over the bed, the two chairs arranged next to the fire, and the stacks of books on a shelf near the door. "This is comfortable."

"It is, isn't it?" she agreed. "One thing that can be said for Lady Burton is that she does an excellent job seeing to all the needs of her guests."

His gaze finally stopped searching, softening when it came to rest on her.

"Come here," he said, holding out his hands, and she readily stepped into them, her lips curling upward at the tenderness in his gaze, although there was more lurking in the depths of his stare.

Hunger.

"I came to you because I couldn't stay away," he said in a low voice. "But I promise I will not succumb to temptation with you tonight."

"Why not if we are going to be married?" she asked, inching closer. Their bodies were lined up flush against one another, Noelle's head tilted so that her nose rested beneath his lips.

"Because I want to do this properly," he said. "Even if everyone thinks we have been together, *we* know the truth. I will marry you, and I will have a proper wedding night with you."

"Well, look at you, ever the gentleman," she teased. "I am happy to be with you now, but if you prefer to wait, I think I can summon the patience."

Her fingers curled around his neck, playing with the collar of the wrapper he had borrowed from his hosts and the silky hairs swirling over it.

He reached down, lifting her legs around his hips, then walked her over to one of the wide wingback chairs in front of the fire, drawing her close.

"It will be worth it," he said, although his voice was huskier than usual. "I promise."

"For a man who is intent on waiting, you have an odd way of showing it," she said, arching an eyebrow, for he was only piquing her desire. Perhaps he was doing it on purpose.

"I know," he said, raising one hand and running it over

her hair. The movement was innocent yet so sensual. "I did want to talk to you."

"As I wanted to speak with you," she said. "So much happened today, and yet we hardly ever had a moment alone."

"Because you just had to walk with Lord John."

She leaned back, her eyes widening at the hardness in his gaze as he said it. "Why, Cooper, were you jealous?"

"No," he said gruffly, although he averted her eyes, which she kept upon him until he finally relented. "Fine. I was jealous. Even though I know that I have nothing to worry about. Can you blame me for wanting to be the man with you on his arm?"

She leaned down until her forehead was resting against his. "You are right. You have nothing to worry about. I wanted to walk with Lord John to see if he would impart any information that might be helpful. Sometimes, a man is more likely to be open with an unthreatening young woman than he would be with a man he considers a rival – or more."

"That is smart," he acquiesced. "Did you learn anything?"

"I did learn that a card game was being played the night of the murder – or so he said. Lord Northbridge left the gathering."

"Did any of the rest of them leave at the same time?" he asked, suddenly interested, and she nodded grimly.

"Apparently, they all did at some point. Lord Northbridge said he had a matter to deal with, so they all decided to take a break. Some went for a drink, others to collect cheroots to smoke, and some went to bed."

"That doesn't narrow it down."

"It might come out in the inquiry tomorrow."

"That should be interesting."

"Let's hope it will be finished with quickly." Noelle leaned back, the thought that had been bothering her resurfacing.

"Do you truly think that we are currently living with a killer? Could anyone else be at risk?"

He sighed, tucking loose tendrils of her hair behind her ear.

"I do not know for certain, although I promise I will keep you safe."

Her heart warmed, the heat spreading through the rest of her body. "You are sweet."

He laughed. "No one has ever called me that before."

"Well," she said with a shrug, "I am happy to be the first."

"Amongst everything else that was going on, I did speak to Lord Burton. He is happy to have us marry during the house party. In fact, Lady Burton, apparently, is thrilled about our nuptials."

"So I heard," Noelle said, laughing as she remembered the woman rushing up to her in gratitude that Noelle was saving their house party.

"Lord Burton agreed to accompany us and your father to see the vicar. Lord Aster also has connections that he believes should help. I see no reason we couldn't marry on Christmas Eve."

Her heart pounded rapidly at the thought, and her fingers tightened on Cooper's hair. She was going to be married – to him. Such a wild idea, especially when she had thought she had lost all chance of marriage with her father's debts.

She spread her hands over his face, which he opened to her. Despite the expectation that she would one day find a husband, the act of being so intimate with a man had never occurred to Noelle. But here he was, open to her, willing to do whatever it took to keep her safe and happy.

And he didn't even love her.

She ran her fingers over his temples and his jaw, her thumbs over his prominent cheekbones before dipping down to his neck and collarbone. She shoved aside his wrapper, pleased to find his chest bare beneath it.

"Noelle," he said, although he closed his eyes as pleasure ran over his face, and he didn't stop her. "What are you doing?"

"I want to touch you. Explore you. Is that all right?"

"Of course," he said, although his throat bobbed as he was obviously affected by what she was doing. Good. That was her point entirely.

She trailed kisses along his chest, mapping out every inch of him with reverence. His muscles relaxed as she explored, and she reveled in the power she could hold over a man who was usually so intimidatingly powerful himself.

Cooper's fingers finally found their place, tentatively threading through her hair as if seeking an anchor in the storm of sensations she was stirring within him. His touch sent shivers down her spine, and suddenly waiting to be together for another five days was a silly suggestion, despite how sweet it was.

Without hesitation, she let her mouth follow where her fingers had been, tasting the salt of his skin as his scent washed over her, inviting her closer.

While she might have started with gentleness, Noelle's touch grew in boldness, leaving a trail of tender kisses down Cooper's chest, each touch causing the tension between them to string ever tighter. His steady breaths turned ragged as her exploration ventured lower, his body lifting toward her as she went.

When she reached the waistband of the trousers he still wore below his wrapper, Cooper's grip on her tightened with silent urgency. His jaw tensed and he shook his head. "None of that. Not yet."

"Why—"

"You come first."

Without another word, he lifted her effortlessly in his arms and carried her to the bed, laying her down gently before him as the canopy framed his head and his delicious body, now uncovered by the wrapper that had fallen off on the way. Their eyes locked in a shared hunger, a mutual understanding passing between them in the charged air of the room.

Noelle's heart thundered in her chest as Cooper hovered over her, his gaze intense and unwavering until he leaned down to capture her lips in a searing kiss.

"I think waiting is a mistake," she panted when he finally came up for air. "I think—"

"We will still wait to come together completely," he growled. "But that doesn't mean we cannot enjoy ourselves in the meantime."

He untied her wrapper, which she hadn't even realized was still cinched tight around her. She slid her arms out of it before eagerly lifting her nightgown over her head until she was naked in front of him. She knew she should feel exposed, shy perhaps, but Cooper made her feel that she had nothing to fear, that he would accept her as she was without judgment.

Which was more attractive than anything else she could imagine.

When she lifted her gaze to his face, she couldn't help but grin despite the desire coursing through her body. His eyes were wide, his lips slightly parted as he stared at her, and Noelle could say with certainty that she had never felt more beautiful than she did in this moment.

"Noelle," he said in a choked voice. "You are… exquisite. I am a lucky, lucky man."

She reached a hand up, needing him closer. "I would have said that I am the lucky one."

With that, he shook his head as he trailed feather-light

kisses down her neck, leaving a trail of fire in his wake. Noelle's breath hitched as his hands skimmed the sensitive skin of her stomach, tracing the curve of her hips and thighs. She arched into his touch, desperate for more.

Cooper looked up, his eyes meeting hers, burning with hunger and desire as he continued his journey down her body. Everywhere his lips touched was set ablaze, a warm tingling sensation radiating through every inch of her being. She felt boneless beneath him, anchored to the bed as he leaned overtop of her, keeping his entire body weight from her on his arms bracketing her body.

He kissed her belly button and then delved lower still until he reached her inner thighs. Noelle's heart pounded furiously against her ribs, excitement coursing through her veins as she watched him approach the edge of forbidden territory.

"Cooper," she whispered, that hesitancy that had been absent suddenly invading. "Should you do this?"

"Oh yes," he said with a wicked grin. "I most definitely should."

And with that, he dipped his head, his hot breath skating over her most intimate places. She shuddered, tensing at the unexpected shiver that shot through her, uncertain of what to expect but trusting that he would keep her safe. He had in every other way, had he not?

He kissed her again, this time more firmly. A whimper escaped her lips as tendrils of pleasure began to uncoil within her. She wasn't entirely sure what she was supposed to be doing, what was to come, but she closed her eyes and allowed herself to follow the sensations he set. Cooper continued his barrage of kisses and licks, slowly inching lower until he finally reached his destination.

With a devilish grin on his face, he used his tongue to part her folds gently, tasting her in a way that she hadn't even known was possible. The awareness of his warm breath on her most secret parts was overwhelming as he continued to explore.

At first, she tensed, concerned of what he might think of her, but at the way he worshipped every part of her body with such reverence and care, she soon let that go. Once she relaxed, she was taken aback by the sensations that surged through her, and her hips arched off the bed involuntarily as wave upon wave of pleasure washed over her.

He backed off but never left her, and when Noelle finally returned to herself, he was lying next to her with a self-satisfied smile on his face.

"Did you enjoy yourself?" he asked, laughter teasing the corners of his mouth, and when he leaned in, she swatted him away.

"You know I did," she said, before noting just how dark his eyes were, reminding her that his own desire was yet to be satiated. "But you haven't yet."

"Oh, I enjoyed myself just fine," he said. "Do not worry your pretty face over that."

"Are you going to…" she swallowed as she waved a hand at him, "…do something about that?"

"Yes," he said cautiously.

"Can I watch?"

His eyes widened before he nodded his head nearly imperceptibly.

"You could watch… or help."

Suddenly she wanted nothing else.

CHAPTER 18

Cooper had not intended this when he had entered Noelle's room.

He had only wanted to talk to and spend time with her.

Which was an odd sensation in itself.

His family had never been particularly close, and he had lost his mother early. They were too busy trying to survive in any way possible to be sitting around the fire in entertaining games.

He had spent most of his childhood stealing from other people – a fact that he had yet to share with Noelle, although he suspected that she had already guessed that some of his past was slightly nefarious.

He watched her, this beautiful, well-bred woman, lean in and unfasten his trousers before pushing them lower until his erection sprang free. Her eyes widened, her mouth rounding, and he wondered if he had shocked her.

"Is this too much?" he asked, barely able to voice the words.

"No," she said. "This is... *more* than enough. But I'm still interested."

"I'm glad to hear it," he said as he lowered his hand and wrapped it around his cock, slowly stroking as he watched her. She didn't even need to be doing anything. Just sitting there with her pink lips slightly parted and those brown eyes round and curious was nearly enough to send him over the edge.

Then she reached her hand toward him.

"Can I do it?"

"I certainly couldn't say no to that," he choked out.

"Will you show me how?"

"I'd be glad to."

She was hesitant at first as her graceful hand replaced his. He placed his overtop, noting how pale her skin appeared next to his darker one, her hand tiny beneath his, before he began moving it up and down, slowly at first so that he could enjoy it, until he became overwhelmed by sensations.

Eventually, he threw his head back, closing his eyes, allowing her to take over.

She was certainly an eager learner, and soon enough, he was coming over her, spending on her stomach as she gasped, the tip of her tongue peeking out as she licked her lips in excitement, watching him.

"Noelle," he said, just managing to hold himself up. "That was…"

"I know," she said with a smile, and after a couple of moments, he collected himself to find linen and clean her up, doing so nearly reverently.

"You are a gem," he said, stretching out beside her. "I don't deserve you. You know that, right?"

"I wish you would stop saying that," she said. "For it is not at all true."

He paused, uncertain how much he should share with her, but if she was going to be his wife, she needed to know everything.

"I have done things in my past that I am not proud of."

"Haven't we all?"

"Yes, but…" Best just to come out with it. "I stole. Pick-pocketed at first."

"That explains the lock picking," she said before lifting her hand to his face. "But you do not steal anymore, do you?"

"No," he said, resting his head in her palm. "I was… enter-prising as a boy. At first, I led a group of other children in pickpocketing. After my mother died – of a sickness that I survived – I knew that wouldn't be enough. I began to buy what others considered old junk. I'd fix it and sell it. It was my first business, along with fighting for coin. As I made money, I invested a little where I could. I knew who I wanted to be and where to get to, so I taught myself how to move in those circles. I changed my accent, learned manners, and hired experts in areas I knew nothing about – like danc-ing. I was lucky, but I also worked hard. I've always had a knack for knowing what – and who – to bet on. I seldom lost."

"Until this railroad deal."

He nodded. "I no longer believe that Sanderson ran off with the money. I think something happened to him."

"By the same person who killed Lord Northbridge?"

Cooper nodded as Noelle, as bright as she was, began to tie all the threads together.

"Now it is known that you want to follow through with a venture for the same railroad."

"Yes."

"So, you could be in danger."

"I could be, but that is not my concern. I can take care of myself. I have for years. A person couldn't survive in my neighborhood if he couldn't defend himself. It is you that I am worried about."

"There would be nothing to gain by coming after me."

"Unless it is to get to me," he said. "All I ask is that you are careful, and you do not go anywhere alone."

"It's hard to be alone when this man follows me everywhere I go…" She began to laugh, and he shook his head as his own chuckle coursed through him.

"I am becoming slightly infatuated, I must admit that," he said, staring at her as the pieces of what he felt began to fall together. He desired this woman with everything within him. He wanted to be married to her. When he wasn't with her, he couldn't wait until the next time he would be. He… good God, was he in love with her?

If he was, he had to take care.

She could never love a man like him, meaning he had to guard his emotions carefully. If she knew the depths of his feelings for her, she would likely pity him.

His expression must have changed, for she pushed herself up from the bed, her own gaze shuttering.

"Thank you for sharing that with me."

"I want you to know who I truly am before we marry. I never want you to regret anything."

"I cannot see a world in which I would regret marrying you," she said softly from beneath hooded eyes, causing his heart to jump.

"After learning all of this, you still want me?" How could she?

"Even more."

"That is more than I deserve," he said before pressing a kiss against her lips. "Can I stay with you tonight?"

"For my safety?" she asked, meeting his gaze, her expression strangely vulnerable.

"Yes," he said. "But also… just because I do not want to leave you."

Her lips lifted shyly, her eyelids dropping. "I would love that."

As he curled around her, her back against his front, Cooper wondered how his life had changed so abruptly.

Yes, he had luck in business, but people didn't stay with him. That was why he had always put his energy into his financial endeavors—they never disappointed him and left him in control for the most part.

He was trying to trust Noelle's not running away, which was never a sure thing—even if she had the best intentions.

Which was why he was now awaiting the inevitable — for reality to come crashing down.

When it did, it was going to hurt. Agonizingly.

But for the first time, he felt ready to take that risk.

* * *

THEY WERE all assembled in the drawing room late the next morning, seated on various pieces of furniture as well as chairs that had been brought in from the library to line the side of the room.

Cooper entered the room after Noelle and walked straight toward where she sat on the plush burgundy sofa resting against the wall beneath angelic landscape paintings of the Cornish countryside.

Noelle couldn't help the smile that graced her lips at the sight of him despite the circumstances, and when he sat next to her, she slipped her hand into his. He tucked her in close to his side and she snuggled into him, taking the comfort he silently offered. How had she not realized just what a good man he was? She knew that he wasn't proud of his upbringing, but it had made him into the man he was today, so for that, she could find no fault.

Her father walked in and nodded a greeting to them. Noelle knew that he had agreed to this marriage due to its financial implications, but she appreciated that he was also accepting of Cooper despite the differences between their backgrounds.

"This feels like we should be posing for a Christmas portrait," Noelle whispered to Cooper, who couldn't help but grin. This arrangement seemed so odd and out of place that Noelle almost felt like laughing at the absurdity. Lord Burton glanced their way as though sensing her misplaced amusement before striding to the front of the room as another stranger joined them.

"Good morning, everyone," Lord Burton greeted them. "Today was supposed to be a day of sledding, but we have something different on the agenda, what with... recent circumstances."

Lord and Lady Burton's attempt at normalcy would have been humorous if it wasn't so sad.

"You will remember Mr. Briggs, the coroner. He examined the body and the location where Lord Northbridge was found. Lord Northbridge will, of course, have a proper funeral. His sister, Lady Jennifer, has asked that his body be transported to his home parish. She will depart after today's inquiry."

"Oh, my good heavens," Lady Burton said, fanning herself from her place on the chair beside Lord Burton. Lady Aster and Lady Crupley also looked ill at ease, while the younger women seemed more resigned to the situation. "This is all too much."

"We will do our best to have this taken care of as quickly as possible," Mr. Briggs said. "I understand this is Christmastide, but a man has lost his life. We must do this properly."

"Of course, Mr. Briggs," Lord Burton said with a nod, although his expression belied his true feelings before he turned to the group before him. "The coroner's jury – which he assured me is necessary although I had hoped that it wouldn't be – will be assembled in the side of this room."

He waved to the dining room chairs set in front of them, facing them as though they were for an audience who would be watching them onstage. Noelle supposed that would be precisely what it would feel like.

"Are there any questions before we begin?"

"How long will this take?" Hermione asked as Hattie sniffed loudly beside her.

"It depends on how much information there is to impart," Mr. Briggs said. "We will ask you to leave the room, and then we will interview each of you and the servants, one at a time."

"Are we suspects?" Lord John demanded, standing abruptly.

"Our main purpose here today is to determine whether or not this was a murder," Mr. Briggs said. "Due to the circumstances as well as the request to expedite the process before Christmas, the magistrate will also be in attendance to determine if anyone is at fault in case this does conclude to be a murder."

Lady Burton let out a moan at that before covering her mouth while Hattie sobbed again.

"Very well," Lord Burton sighed. "We appreciate your discretion in the matter. We have food set out in the dining room and card games in the adjoining parlor to play while we each await to be called. I will be assisting Mr. Briggs."

Lord Burton stood beside Mr. Briggs in the room as the rest of them filed out. Noelle wrapped her arm around Cooper's elbow, and as they exited the room, she couldn't help but hear Mr. Briggs telling Lord Burton that, no, he could not stay in the room to listen to the testimony. Cooper's lips were pressed into a firm line, and she could tell he was also intrigued about what would transpire. But they couldn't exactly listen in without raising suspicion.

She tried to steal a glance at Cooper, but he was too busy

craning his head around the room, although she had no idea what he could be looking for.

"Mr. Hartwell," Mr. Briggs said, stopping their progress. "Why do we not begin with you?"

Cooper's mouth quirked into a wry grin, but he showed no outward sign of annoyance.

"Very well," he said. "Where would you like me?"

"On the sofa in the middle," Mr. Briggs said, and Noelle squeezed his arm before following Hattie into the dining room.

She agreed with Lord Burton on one thing. She would also like this over as quickly as possible.

She just hoped that it wouldn't end with an accusation against Cooper. He must remember the story they had agreed upon.

It was the only way out.

CHAPTER 19

*N*oelle tapped her foot impatiently as she set another puff pastry into her mouth while Hattie watched her with wide eyes. The young women present – Noelle, Hattie, Hermione, Brighton, and Lady Jennifer, who had just joined them – sat together in one corner of the room.

While Hattie's eyes remained rimmed in red and her sniffles had yet to abate, Lady Jennifer was surprisingly collected for a woman who had lost her brother potentially to murder.

"How are you holding up, Jennifer?" Noelle asked, which caused Hattie to let out another hiccup.

"Fine," she said in her usual one-word answer.

"Do you truly think it is best to take his body home?" Hermione asked, posing her question in that headlong way that only Hermione could.

"He would have wanted to be buried close to my parents," Jennifer said, while Noelle sat back and assessed her, wondering if, perhaps, Jennifer had another reason for wanting to remove the body from the investigation – and distance herself from it as well. On the other hand, Noelle could understand not wanting to be surrounded by reminders of what had happened.

"When will you leave?" Noelle asked.

"This afternoon, if possible," she said. "The weather is still clear, so we might as well."

Noelle nodded absentmindedly, her mind still on Cooper and the current questioning. She wondered if they would ask her next, concerned that they shouldn't have time to coordinate their stories. Of course, it was too late for that.

"How many pastries are you going to eat?" Brighton asked Noelle, watching her pick up another Chelsea bun. She couldn't help that she ate too much – particularly sweets – when she was nervous.

"Does it matter?" Noelle asked.

"You're not married yet," Brighton said, looking down her nose at Noelle, who rolled her eyes. Cooper had seemed more than happy with the curvier parts of her body, although she wouldn't supply Brighton with any more information to gossip about.

"Which begs the question," Hermione said, leaning forward, "Are you marrying so quickly because you have no other choice?" Her eyes flicked down to Noelle's stomach and then back up.

"No," Noelle said around her pastry. "Not at all. We are marrying quickly because we truly *want* to be married and want to do this properly. It seemed a perfect time with family and friends already gathered."

"Not *his* friends," Hermione commented.

"No," Noelle said, guilt filling her that she hadn't considered that yet. "Not his friends. Perhaps we can have another ceremony when we return to London."

"It's just unusual, is all," Hermione said with a shrug, and

Noelle had to force her smile as she tamped down what she would honestly like to say.

"I understand," she said. "However, your mother seemed quite happy for us to be married here, which I appreciate, as I no longer have my mother to look out for me."

That caused Hermione to stop talking. What retort could she offer?

Noelle gritted her teeth, ready to change the subject, when Cooper walked in. His eyes went straight to her, and he gave her the most imperceptible nod as though to tell her everything was all right.

Before they could speak, Lord Burton walked in and requested her presence.

She had been right.

She squeezed Cooper's hand as she walked by him, her heart racing at the thought of what was to come. She didn't have anything to hide and hoped that having men without titles on the jury would remove the disadvantage he faced among the noble set.

Still, she couldn't help clenching her hands tightly in her lap when she took the seat on the sofa, trying to take comfort in its warmth as she reminded herself that Cooper had sat here minutes before, that he was close by, and that she wasn't truly alone.

She raised her eyes to the twelve men sitting in front of her, who ranged from laborers to artisans to merchants from the nearby Guilford – at least, from what she guessed based on their dress.

They were all staring at her with frank curiosity, and she tried to manage a smile to appear friendlier.

Mr. Briggs sat in front of them, pen and paper on his lap, while another man, white-haired with a bushy white beard, who she assumed was the magistrate, sat to the other side of the room, away from the jury.

"Lady Noelle, thank you for speaking to us."

She nodded, biting her tongue so she wouldn't tell them it wasn't as though she'd had much choice.

"We are trying to ascertain what occurred the night Lord Northbridge died," Mr. Briggs said. "Can you please tell us when you last saw the victim?"

"Of course," she said demurely. "It was at dinner that evening. We ate together, and then the ladies retired to the drawing room. The gentlemen joined us after an hour or so. Some began to play cards, and when I retired for the evening, Lord Northbridge was still there, as were all of the men he was playing with."

"Very good. Do you remember what the men were speaking about?"

"I was not close enough to hear."

"When you retired for the night, did Mr. Hartwell accompany you?"

"Not immediately," she said, hoping Cooper said the same. "My lady's maid helped me prepare for bed. I tried to sleep but was having difficulty, so… I went to speak with my fiancée."

Her cheeks burned red, even though she knew she had nothing to be embarrassed about. Still, she had no idea what these men would think of her, nor who they would tell of her actions.

But this was worth it if it meant protecting Cooper.

"He was in the room when you entered?" Mr. Briggs asked, showing no emotion.

"He was," she confirmed. "He opened the door for me and allowed me in."

"What did you do?"

She lifted her chin. "That, Mr. Briggs, is of no business to anyone in this room. Suffice it to say that I was with him and that neither of us left."

There was a low murmuring among the jury, while Mr. Briggs glanced over to the magistrate, who waved him forward, obviously accepting her answer.

"Very well," he grumbled, showing his first bit of annoyance. "How long did you remain in the room?"

"I would suppose it was less than an hour, although I lost track of time," she said, biting her lip, hoping that her expected throes of passion would forgive her uncertainty over how long she was supposed to have been in the room with Cooper. "I was there when we heard the noise from outside the window."

"Explain the noise, please."

"It sounded like a gunshot," she said. "Which, I suppose it was."

"How many gunshots did you hear?"

"We heard the first right away," she said. "The second was delayed but sounded a few moments later."

"What did Mr. Hartwell do at this time?"

"He looked out the window, but he couldn't see anything," she said, remembering the story they had discussed last night before falling asleep. "He then put on his wrapper and told me to stay in the room while he went to see what had happened."

"What did you do?"

"I did what he said. I stayed in the room. When I heard noise out the window, I looked out to see what was happening below me, but I couldn't see anything properly until Lord Burton stepped outside with the lantern and cast light on everything."

"What did you see then?"

"Coop—Mr. Hartwell had fallen over Lord Burton's body."

"How was he reacting?"

"He was shocked, from what I could tell," she said.

"Then you stayed in the bedroom?"

"When I saw other guests emerging into the night and heard ladies in the corridor, I joined them," she said. "Mr. Hartwell had asked me to stay so I would be safe, but I assumed all would be fine once we gathered as a group."

"Do you have any reason to suspect that Mr. Hartwell might have wanted to kill Lord Northbridge?"

Noelle swallowed hard before tightening her fingers around one another and squeezing her knees together as she sat as tall as possible.

"It is no secret that Mr. Hartwell and Lord Northbridge did not get along well," she said, knowing that the story would come out, so she might as well tell her version of the events, as damning as it might be. "Lord Northbridge was forceful with me earlier the evening before. Mr. Hartwell saved me from him and his threats," she said, having to clear her throat, surprised at the emotion telling the story that arose within her.

"They had words," she continued. "However, Mr. Hartwell is not the type of man who would ever kill someone."

"What do you know of Mr. Hartwell's background?"

Perspiration broke out on Noelle's brow, which she hoped would not be evident to the men seated before her.

"Not a great deal," she admitted. "I know that his family was slightly impoverished when he was young, but he worked hard to become the man he is today."

"Do you have any other reason to suspect him?"

"Not at all," Noelle said firmly. "He is a good man, Mr. Briggs. I would not be marrying him otherwise."

She hoped that the confidence she had infused in her voice, the conviction she felt, would come across to these men and cause them to believe in her.

"Very well, Lady Noelle. You are free to go," Mr. Briggs

said upon what appeared to be approval from the magistrate in the corner.

Lord Burton was waiting outside the door – likely listening at the keyhole, if Noelle had to guess – and escorted her to the parlor, where most of the guests were now congregated, at least so it seemed from the piano music floating toward the drawing room.

She found no sign of Cooper, but her father greeted her, worry on his face.

"Noelle," he said, placing his hands on her arms. "How are you?"

"I'm fine, Father, truly," she assured him before lowering her voice and looking around to ensure no one was listening to them. "My greatest concern is that Cooper will be blamed for this simply because he is not considered one of us."

"Well," her father said, squaring his usually stooped shoulders back, "he will be my son-in-law soon, which makes him part of our family. And I do not want to see anyone in our family hurt."

"Thank you, Father," she said, blinking away the tears that threatened. "That means more than you know."

He patted her arm somewhat awkwardly, clearly unsure of how to show his affection for her, but she appreciated it all the same.

"Have you seen Cooper?" she asked, looking around, and her father frowned.

"He followed you out when it was time for your inquiry," he said. "I assumed he would wait and return with you."

"No," she said, tapping her fingers together. "I believe he considers himself something of a private investigator in this matter. I'm sure he'll return shortly."

"Hopefully," her father murmured. "We cannot create any further cause for suspicion."

"Cooper seems to know what he's doing," she said with confidence that she didn't entirely feel. "I'm sure of it."

Or, at least, she hoped.

She had fallen for a man for the first time in her life.

She wasn't about to allow him to become convicted of murder.

CHAPTER 20

"*T*here you are."

A pang of guilt coursed through Cooper at the relief on Noelle's face. He hadn't meant to leave her in the dark all day, but he hadn't been able to risk anyone finding out what he was doing.

"Where were you?" Noelle strode up to him, her tone worried not accusatory, clasping his hands in hers as she stared into his face inquiringly. "It has been hours. They are finishing the inquest now."

"I know," he said, looking around the parlor before taking her hand and tugging it to lead her toward the door. "Let's go for another walk?"

She shivered. "While I love the outdoors, today is far too cold."

"I know. Why do we not try the ballroom? There are so many trees in there we shall feel as though we are outside but without the chill."

"That sounds just fine to me," she said as he led her through the halls. He stopped her along the way anytime he saw mistletoe, turning her toward him to place quick yet firm kisses on her lips. They were no longer trying to avoid the kissing bough, but instead, he seemed to be actively walking them along a path as though he had mapped out where each piece of the greenery could be found.

When they entered, the ballroom was dark, and the sun was setting beyond the windows. Cooper found a candelabra and lifted it to lead their way as the fire across the room was so dim that it only cast the room in shadows.

"This all seems rather clandestine," she teased, and he squeezed her arm. Instead of linking arms as they would in public, he looped his arm around her, holding her close against him.

"I missed you," he said, kissing her temple, surprising himself with his admission. She leaned into him, closing her eyes as she savored his closeness.

"As I missed you," she said. "It is hard to believe that we barely knew one another until a couple of months ago, isn't it?"

"It certainly is," he agreed, "although I wonder if my life is one you would enjoy. I hope you will be happy when we return to London."

"Why would I not be?" she asked, lifting a brow. "I will be with you."

"My home is fine enough, although I spend most of my time working. My life has always been about business, about getting ahead. I'm not sure I could ever be enough," he sighed. "But I will most certainly try."

Before Noelle could assure him once more that there was nothing to concern himself with, that he deserved all the love anyone could give him, he began to explain his absence that afternoon.

"When we were in the drawing room, I was looking around the walls and noted a few areas that did not appear to have the correct dimensions for where the adjacent room should stop and start," he said. "In a manor like this, especially one in which the family hosts so often, I wondered if there could be a servants' passageway beside it. It didn't take long to find it."

She stopped, turning to him in surprise. "You listened to the inquiry?"

"I did," he said, and it was his turn to jump when she swatted him.

"Why didn't you come find me? I would have loved to join you!"

"I know, but I found it while you were being interviewed, and then I worried I would be seen leaving and re-entering if I came to tell you," he said. "Besides that, it was a long afternoon. I was hungry. Thirsty, too."

"Was it worth it?" she asked.

"Yes and no," he said with a sigh. "I couldn't hear everything perfectly. Everyone interviewed was guarded, as expected, and not much new information came to light."

"Did they describe the card game?"

"They did," he confirmed. "Taking part that evening was Lord Northbridge, Lord John, Lord Rochester, Lord Andrew, and Lord Bingly."

"Lord Bingly," she said, snapping her fingers. "I always forget about him."

"He is rather forgettable," Cooper agreed. "They played for a time, and then Lord Northbridge excused himself, as Lord John told you. It seemed the game broke up after that, and they all went their separate ways, except for Lord Rochester and Lord Andrew, who walked upstairs together as their rooms were beside one another."

"Yes, but they would be just as inclined to vouch for one another as you and I would."

"True," he agreed. "The ladies were all distraught and told the same story. They retired for the night and didn't leave their bedchambers until they heard the commotion. Some of them heard the shots. Lady Hattie also commented on seeing you emerge from my bedchamber, which confirmed our story."

He eyed her mischievously. "Which leads me to ask you, my lady, what *were* you doing in my bedchamber?"

"Watching you out the window," she said. "You said to stay inside but didn't say I had to stay in my bedroom."

"You do not do what you're told, do you?"

"What are you going to do about it?" she asked, sidling toward him, and he lowered his head.

"You would like to know, would you?"

She lifted a brow.

"Well, I—"

"Mr. Hartwell!"

They jumped apart at the voice in the doorway, turning as one to see Lord Burton standing there disapprovingly.

"The coroner would like to see us all. He has made his decision."

Noelle and Cooper exchanged a glance.

This was it. Cooper knew the chances were still high that he was going to be named a murderer – or, at least, suspected of being one. If that happened, he would lose either his reputation or his life.

He refused to bring Noelle down with him. If he were accused, this would be the last she would ever see of him – even if she didn't know it yet.

In just a few moments, they would find out whether this entire thing between them was finished before it had even started.

* * *

Noelle couldn't stop the bouncing of her knee. Cooper smoothed his hand over her thigh as they all had returned to their places in the tableau, and she studied him, wondering how he could be so calm.

She was not a woman overly given to panic or histrionics, but she couldn't help the nerves that had built within her at this moment.

The jury had departed, leaving only the coroner and the magistrate, who stood before them along with Lord Burton.

"First, I would like to thank you all for your cooperation today," said the coroner, Mr. Briggs. "I know this is not an ideal situation."

There was a murmuring of agreement among the guests before he continued.

"I know you are all most eager to learn what happened. I will not waste any more of your time. We have determined that this was, indeed, a murder."

A few gasps sounded, and Noelle had to stop herself from rolling her eyes. They all knew this was a murder. One didn't accidentally walk outside and shoot a man in the middle of the chest with a pistol.

"That is all from me," the coroner said. "The magistrate has a few words to say about his suppositions and his role in all of this."

This was what had most terrified Noelle.

The magistrate slowly stood, pacing back and forth as he eyed them all one at a time as though taking their measure and trying to determine just who was the culprit.

"Most of the testimony we heard today was polished and precise," he said, his disdain for the nobility evident. Interesting. "Almost as though it was practiced ahead of time."

Of course it was practiced. They'd had two days to prepare for this inquiry. Noelle and Cooper had determined their story, and they were not even at fault.

"The servants helped as they had the most valid form of events. They know all of the comings and goings throughout the house. It would be wise for you to know what they see."

Noelle swallowed hard at the accusation. The magistrate wasn't wrong, although she did feel like Cooper always had an appreciation for the servants.

"After the conclusion of the card game, Lord North-bridge was seen coming out of a wing of the house where he did not have a bedroom," the magistrate said as he continued his pacing, clearly enjoying the opportunity to hold them all in a captive audience. "Which, of course, tells us that he was visiting someone in that wing. A young lady, perhaps?"

Hattie gasped, although Noelle wasn't sure whether it was for show or whether she was as surprised as the rest of them. She was sure it was Hermione, but she didn't want any part in that sisterly squabble.

"All of the ladies present were accounted for in their bedrooms, according to their lady's maids, and none were seen wandering the hallways. Which begs the question, just *who* did Lord Northbridge visit? And did that cause jealousy among any other guests – man or woman?"

The atmosphere changed as everyone in the room began shifting back and forth in their seats, clearly uneasy, wondering if they were a suspect or sitting next to a poten-tial killer.

Noelle knew she could trust Cooper and her father. She was also reasonably certain Hattie didn't have a violent bone in her body. As for everyone else… well, it remained to be seen, although she wasn't sure she could trust the magistrate to have correctly determined the culprit. She had far more faith in Cooper's sleuthing.

He understood people in a way that most didn't, while the magistrate seemed more interested in proving to them how smart he considered himself to be – whereas Cooper needed no pretending.

"We can piece together what happened following his emergence. Servants saw a few men in various places of the manor, although none were near Lord Northbridge. Did one of them see him leaving this young lady's bedroom?"

He lifted a finger in the air. "Then, finally, we have the missing piece of the puzzle. The pistol. It was found in the bedroom of one gentleman. None other than…" He held the finger aloft as he stopped, looking from one side of the room to the other dramatically as they all waited, breath held together. "Lord Bingly!"

They all turned to stare at Lord Bingly, whose pale face became even paler than usual. His dark freckles stood out, and his mouth opened and closed a few times before he finally found words.

"Pistol? I do not even own a pistol!"

It was true that he certainly didn't seem the type of man who would cause any form of violence. Then again, one never knew the truth about others for sure.

"Then how did it end up in your room?"

"It must have been planted there!" he said. "I had no ill intentions toward Lord Northbridge."

"That's true. That could have happened," the magistrate said, stroking his chin. "But for now, it is the only evidence we have."

"What of the young lady?" Lord Bingly said, struggling for words like a fish thrown on shore. "I had no designs on any young lady here; I can promise you that."

A few eyes were cast downward at that as it appeared that other gentlemen could not say the same.

"From what I was told, Lord Northbridge and Lady Hattie had an understanding, but Lady Hattie had no… relations with the man," the magistrate said. "However, it seems that Lady Hermione might have."

Hattie let out a cry as she stared at her sister. "Hermione?"

"I did nothing!" Hermione objected crossly, although she didn't outright deny it. "Who would say such a thing?"

"I will not reveal my sources," said the magistrate. "I also heard that he had a past with Lady Noelle."

Noelle's insides froze as she felt all of the stares on her, although none were heavier than Cooper's.

"That is not entirely true," she managed.

"What does that mean?" Cooper asked in a low, dangerous voice.

"He kissed me once when I first had my come out. I allowed it to happen, but it was just one time, and it was in a public setting."

"How could you? I thought we were friends!" Hattie cried, and Noelle sighed, wishing this had never come to light, for it had meant absolutely nothing. In fact, it had turned her off of Lord Northbridge, allowing him to be open to Hattie – but how was she supposed to tell her friend that?

"It was three years ago, Hattie, before you and Lord Northbridge had any understanding. We decided from there that we had no further interest in one another."

Well, she had decided. But telling Hattie she was the second choice right now didn't seem fair.

Cooper had relaxed slightly, although he still opened and closed his hands from fists to palms. Noelle hoped that she wasn't the cause of his ire.

"I guess you didn't hear everything," she murmured, but the conversation continued before he could answer.

"Lady Noelle is right," the magistrate said. "That is in the past. Until evidence shows otherwise, we will assume that Lord Bingly is our suspect. Lord Bingly, we respect your status and will not take you into holding until your trial, which will be in front of the House of Lords. Until then, please remain close to Guilford."

At that, the magistrate marched to the door, leaving the others sitting in their spots as if frozen into statues.

The magistrate's role might have been over, but the evening was not finished.

Far from it.

CHAPTER 21

$\mathcal{D}$ue to the circumstances of the evening and the lateness of the hour, Lord and Lady Burton had suggested a light meal that guests could partake in at their leisure before retiring early.

Thank goodness.

Cooper had taken the opportunity to dress warmly and venture outdoors – alone. He wouldn't make for good company at the moment, not for Noelle or anyone else who risked speaking to him.

He was well aware that he had no reason to be upset with Noelle for a kiss years ago – goodness, he'd had his fair share of experience over the years that had meant nothing – but he was irritated that she had kept it from him.

He was also wondering just what role she had played in it. If Northbridge had forced himself on her in any way, Cooper would like to resurrect him and punch him in the nose all over again.

Then there was the fact that Lord Bingly, although likely as innocent as he proclaimed to be, was left in the manor even though he was suspected of murder. Cooper was well aware that if he had been accused, he would sit in a cold country jail cell, where he would remain for weeks before his trial.

Instead, a lord was offered the opportunity to remain in opulence and perhaps escape or attempt to clear his name.

It almost made Cooper rethink his decision to marry into such a society.

He would have if it weren't for Noelle herself. Was she worth it? Was she who he had thought she was? He had only known her for several weeks but couldn't get enough of her. Even now, if he were across the hall from her bedroom, he likely would have gone over there and shown her what other fun they could have without becoming fully intimate with one another.

He had thought it best to head outside, cool down, and clear his head. He honestly didn't think Bingly had any part in this, but he was still uncertain about who had.

"Stop! You there!"

Cooper sighed. He had hoped that he would be able to spend this time alone, but it seemed that fate had other ideas.

The approaching figure was as dark as the night surrounding them, although his stature was masculine, a cloak billowing behind him. As he approached, Cooper made out the shape of one of the Rochester twins. He guessed Lord Andrew, although he couldn't be sure in this light.

"Hartwell, is that you?"

"It is," Cooper said. "Lord Andrew?"

"Correct!" the twin said as he drew near enough for Cooper to see the grin spread on his face. "Not many people can tell us apart."

"I have a fair mind for names and faces," Cooper said.

"I understand," Lord Andrew said, hands in his pockets as he looked around the gardens. Cooper followed the path through the evergreens and realized they had come far from the house. "Interesting night tonight, wasn't it?"

"It was," Cooper said, wondering why they were chatting as though in the middle of a drawing room during a house party. "What are you doing out here?"

"Taking my nightly walk," Lord Andrew said. "It's part of my regimen to stay healthy. Fresh air and all that."

"I have never heard of that before," Cooper said, eyeing him, wondering if Lord Andrew was having him on.

"It's a new thing," Lord Andrew said. "What brings you to the great outdoors on such a frosty night?"

"Clearing my head," Cooper said, tugging his cap over his ears as the cold started to nip at them.

"Ah, yes, an interesting tidbit of gossip with Lady Noelle and Northbridge. Nothing to concern yourself over, though," Lord Andrew said with a shrug. "I've never seen her so taken with a man as she appears to be with you."

Cooper felt like a young debutante at how that information warmed him through and through.

"What do you make of it all?" he asked, returning the conversation to the murder. "Do you think Bingly has it in him?"

Lord Andrew sighed and placed his hands in his pockets. He breathed out a cloud of smoke into the cold night air and looked off into the distance.

"I've known Bingly a long time," he said, shaking his head. "He's always been the quiet sort. Sometimes, you never know what those ones are thinking, you know?"

Cooper nodded slowly, although there was still something niggling at him, telling him that this wasn't done. The magistrate had been confident in his theory, but he probably would have named anyone as long as he could finish the story in magnificent style and let them all go home in time for Christmas.

Christmas. By then he would be married, his wedding to take place in less than five days.

Cooper could hardly believe it, although that part of his life felt right – unlike this murder investigation.

"What kind of pistol did they find in Bingly's room, did they say?"

"A pepperbox revolver, I'm told."

Interesting. A pepperbox revolver? That couldn't be right. Either Lord Andrew was mistaken, or that pistol had been planted. For the gun that had been fired was most assuredly a percussion cap pistol. Surely, the magistrate would have been competent enough to check... unless he was just looking for a quick win.

"I don't know what to believe about Bingly, although I suppose it's not up to me, now, is it?" Cooper said, lifting a brow. "The coroner and the magistrate have done their job and determined who their man is."

"Whether the House will convict him is another story," Lord Andrew said. "Seems like fairly minimal evidence for such a charge. Chances are he'll be set free."

"Which they probably know," Cooper murmured, understanding dawning. The local authorities had gambled with Lord Bingly's reputation but not his life. They knew that this would never hold. They just wanted this finished and out of their hands, which irritated him to no end. He hated when people didn't take accountability for their responsibilities.

"Probably," Lord Andrew said in his bright, cheery way that Cooper had no issue with unless the subject was as serious as this. "Truth is, I assumed you would be the one they'd pin this on."

"Except I would not have likely walked free, would I have?" Cooper said wryly.

"Probably not," Lord Andrew agreed. "How fortunate you

and Lady Noelle became… familiar before the wedding. Though no one will ever forget it."

"Maybe not," Cooper said. "But we will be married soon enough, so what will it matter?"

"That's true," Lord Andrew said as he turned and began walking to the house, speaking over his shoulder as though assuming Cooper would follow him.

Cooper hesitated. He would have loved to have stayed out longer, but his toes were freezing. He was getting soft in the comfort he had become accustomed to, so far from how he had grown up. "We can hardly believe you were the one she agreed to marry. After Northbridge tried, I think we all took our chance. She's a beauty, but you know that better than anyone. Of course, she's a bit outspoken for many men once they get to know her."

Cooper snorted. These men were idiots. Her intelligence was what he loved most about her.

Love. There was that word again. Coming from him – about a woman. It was disconcerting, to say the least.

"Their loss is my gain," he said as they walked up to the house, their boots crunching on the gravel beneath their feet. The wind swirled around them, and Cooper realized that it was more than just cold air hitting them – there was snow in the air. Would it stick around tonight?

"Well, congratulations to you," Lord Andrew said, extending his hand, and Cooper shook it. "Have a good evening."

He smirked as though knowing what Cooper might be considering for the rest of the night. Only for once, he was wrong.

Cooper had decided that he would give Noelle some space. He had cooled down, yes, and had realized that he wasn't angry at her – he was furious at the thought that Northbridge and men like him had known Noelle for so much longer than he had that he would never have the opportunity to be her first kiss or to have known what she was like as a young girl.

He wasn't in the right frame of mind to spend the night with her, but he was sure that would change by tomorrow.

For what did the past matter? He could be her first in so many other ways. Ways that mattered much more.

He wouldn't just be her first, either.

He would also be her last.

* * *

NOELLE KNEW A LESSER woman would have spent the night tossing and turning, concerned about what her fiancé might think of her and why he had avoided her after learning about a past kiss with another man.

She, on the other hand, slept just fine in the knowledge that she had done nothing wrong, and if Cooper chose to be upset about a kiss that had meant nothing years ago, then so be it.

It was better to learn about his jealousy now than after they were married.

Still, when she opened her door the following day to come face-to-face with him doing the same across the hall, she couldn't ignore the tug of her heart toward him.

She had missed him. That much was certain.

Even if she had nothing to apologize for.

"Good morning," she said, dipping her head.

"Good morning," he said, crossing the corridor in two long steps and coming to a stop in front of her, hands on her shoulders and eyes probing her gaze. "I'm sorry."

"For what?"

"For not providing you assurance last night. I left the drawing room cross and never returned to you because I

174

didn't want to take out any anger on you. But please know…
I was not cross with *you*."

She was relieved to hear that he was not the type of man
who would think otherwise.

"Who were you cross at, then?"

"I was upset with this entire situation – that a man of the
nobility could be charged with nearly no consequence when
it would have been much different for me. I was annoyed
that the magistrate likely had this all wrong. And I was
angry at Northbridge, for I couldn't be certain that he didn't
force himself on you." He paused, searching her face.
"Did he?"

She sighed as she reached up, running her fingers down
the stubble of his jaw.

"He didn't force himself on me, nor was I particularly
eager," she said. "He had called upon me a few times and then
leaned in to kiss me at a party one night. I didn't have much
opportunity to say no, but I didn't push him away either. At
least, not at first."

"But you did?"

"Once I realized that I was not enjoying it, yes." Her lips
quirked up into a smile, for she knew he would enjoy this
next bit of information. "From that experience, I never
wanted to be kissed again."

"Didn't you, now?"

"No. It made me tell Lord Northbridge I was not interested in his courtship. I couldn't imagine having to kiss — or
do more — with him again." She shuddered. "I didn't say
anything to you – or anyone else – about it because it had no
consequence. We both moved on, and when he began
pursuing Hattie, she was so excited that I didn't want to
make her feel like she was a second choice – although I'm a
bit concerned about Hermione's intentions with him."

Cooper looked from one side of the hallway to the other,

ensuring they were alone, before leaning in and wrapping his arms around her, holding her tight.

"You're a good friend," he said, his lips just beside her ear. She tilted her head so he would have better access to her neck. "You're very good in other ways too," he whispered before kissing down it, from below the shell of her ear, until he reached her collarbone. Noelle had to stifle her moan as the desire was nearly instant, overwhelming her. Suddenly, she wanted nothing more than to be alone with Cooper and show him how she felt about him.

"I try to be," she whispered before reaching down and taking his hands, tugging him forward. "Come."

"Into your bedroom?"

She smiled, nodding.

"Do you wish to be kissed now?"

"Do I ever," she said. "Someone showed me that kissing is something to welcome – as long as it is with the right person."

"You are going to break me," he said with a groan, although he allowed her to lead him in.

She didn't know what she was going to do with him.

But she would show him that he had made a mistake ignoring her last night.

CHAPTER 22

*T*his had seemed like such a good idea in the hallway.

But now that they were alone in her bedroom, light streaming in the window allowing no shadow of doubt nor darkness to hide, Noelle began to question herself.

As confident as she usually was, she lost some of it as she wondered exactly what she was supposed to do now.

Fortunately, Cooper didn't seem to have any problem taking over.

He took her mouth rougher than he had before, as though his desire had overcome his usual gentleness. His lips moved over hers, his tongue plundering, as he reached around her and began to undo all of the work her maid had finished just minutes earlier, slipping each button through its hole.

Noelle took that as a sign to undress him in turn, and they fumbled and fought clasps and buttons until Cooper finally took a step back.

"Enough of this," he commanded. "Clothing off."

He helped her undo her remaining buttons and untie her corset. She breathed a sigh of relief as it slipped off again, her gown and all of her garments pooling in a puddle around her feet while he made quick work of his jacket, shirt, and trousers.

She left on her chemise, for there was something she wanted to do – and she would feel just a little less vulnerable if she wasn't completely bare before him.

She knelt in front of his very naked lower half, his cock allowing no room for her to be concerned about just how much he wanted her in turn.

He breathed in deeply, his eyes wide as he stared at her. She met his gaze, silently asking him if this was all right.

"You don't have to do this," he said gruffly, even as his face and body told her that he very much wanted her to.

"I would like to," she said, and he nodded, confusing her when he took her hands in his, lifting her to her feet.

"What's wrong?"

He said nothing as he gathered a blanket from the bed and placed it on the floor beneath her.

"Now you can kneel."

She had to blink away the tears at the care he showed her, even through his haze of desire, as his voice was rough and commanding in that manner he only showed her when they were together in this way. Only when they were alone did he drop the façade, the fabricated accent, and become his true self.

She loved that she had this side of him, a side that no one else ever got to see.

Noelle dropped to her knees on top of the blanket, placing her hands on the front of his thighs as she swallowed hard, hoping that he couldn't see the nerves that suddenly took over her.

"You're so beautiful," he said, running his thumb over her lips, which she parted for him. "So fucking beautiful."

Her eyes widened, as she had never heard such language

178

used in her presence before, but she loved that he wasn't like all of the other men she knew, men who would have treated her like a wife while they saved their raw selves for their mistresses.

She would be both to him.

And now, she needed to know just how to make him happy.

"Can you tell me what to do… please?" she asked, looking up at him with supplication, hoping he would understand what it meant for her to ask this of him.

His jaw ticked, although his expression revealed nothing.

"You have never done this before?"

"Of course not!" she exclaimed. "That kiss with Lord Northbridge was about the extent of my experience."

"No more talk of him – or any other man," he growled. "This is between you and me now – and *only* you and me."

Noelle could only nod, overcome by the possession in his gaze.

"I can't see how you can do any wrong," he said. "As long as you are touching me."

She nodded as she came face-to-face with his cock, unable to look away. Wetness leaked out of the tip, and she tentatively leaned forward and licked it away.

"Fuuuck," he groaned as he ran his hand over her hair, further undoing her maid's work from that morning. He cupped a palm around her head, holding her in position.

"That's it. Use your mouth. How ever you want. How ever feels right."

At first, it felt foreign, uncertain as she licked the side of his manhood, but when his eyes rolled back in his head, she figured she must be doing something right.

"That's it," he encouraged her, his eyes closing. "Like that."

Her confidence grew with his words as she gripped him with one of her hands, using the other on his leg to hold

179

herself up. She licked him from one end do the other as she watched him from beneath her lashes.

Finally, she took him in her mouth completely, sucking him as far as she could.

"Fuck me," he said, and she had never heard so many swears in her entire life, but she considered that meant that she was doing her job well. "Are you sure you've never done this before?"

Since he already knew the answer, she decided not to give him another.

She used her hand to create friction as she sucked him back and forth. He moved with her, and she used her tongue to stroke him inside her mouth further, just as they did when they were kissing.

"I'm going to come, Noelle," he said, pulling out of her mouth and backing away.

She nodded.

"Can I come in your mouth?"

She nodded again, both worried about and anticipating what was happening.

He leaned over, licking his lips before kissing her quickly, then standing and allowing her to take him in her mouth again. Her lips were tight around him as he moved back and forth, holding her head as he set the pace, his need evident by the expression he wore.

"You all right?"

She loved that she could cause such vulnerability within him, making him unravel like this before her, even as he was still concerned for her and ensuring she was doing fine.

"Touch yourself," he commanded, and it took her a minute to realize exactly what he was saying. She reached below her chemise, tentatively touching where she ached for him. She dug her fingers into his legs as he pushed all the way forward, letting out a roar that she was sure could be heard throughout the entire manor as he came into her mouth, and she closed her eyes, revelling that she was the one to do this to him.

She wasn't entirely sure what to do now, but he was there, providing her with linen, cleaning her up as he brought her body flush against his and held her tight against him.

"That was unbelievable," he said roughly into her ear. "Thank you."

"I wanted to make you happy," she said.

"You make me happy just by being with me," he declared. "It's hard to imagine that I ever had a life without you."

He lifted her and placed her on the bed, lifting her chemise as he didn't waste any time in bringing his mouth to her, licking a line down her center where his fingers had been before, causing her hips to lift into the air, searching for harder friction.

Realizing what she needed, he sank his fingers into her, curling them to reach a place that she hadn't known existed as his tongue swirled over a bud of sensitive nerves that had her on edge, riding some precipice that she finally understood was more than worth falling over.

She twirled his fingers into his silky strands of hair as he hummed against her, causing vibrations that had her entire body squirming for more.

"I want this to be good for you," he said as he placed a soft kiss against her, showing her that this was so much more than desire on his part. "Where do you like to be touched?"

"I… I don't know," she said, biting her lip.

"You never touch yourself?"

"No, not really."

"Well, then, I suppose I shall be the one to discover just what works."

He sounded so pleased with himself when he said it that she had to chuckle.

"Do you like circles?" he said, when he moved both his tongue and his fingers over her.

"Yes," she hissed.

"How about back and forth?"

He moved up and down in quick motions.

"Even better," she said as he used his tongue, licking her with pressure.

He moaned himself, and she nearly choked at the thought that he was finding pleasure by giving it to her.

He was urgent yet took his time. Hard yet soft. Relaxed yet persuasive.

He was so handsome that he took her breath away, her body nearly coming off the bed as the vibrations almost overtook her. His mouth never left as he continued, their bodies starting to rock together.

She held onto his hair with one hand, the blankets beneath her with the other.

"Cooper!" she yelled out as the sensations began to rip through her, wave after wave, her eyes meeting his until she had to close them with the force of what was happening to her.

When she finally came down, they lay there together, both panting and completely spent. Cooper curled his fingers around hers, turning on his side to stare into her eyes. She could lose herself in the stormy depths of his, though she figured that someone would come looking for them after a time.

"I could spend all day with you in here," he said, echoing her thoughts.

"I suppose soon we can," she said, her lips curling into a smile, although they stopped when his brow furrowed.

"Yes and no," he said. "A man like me doesn't have all day to lie around and idle the day by. I have to work hard to provide for us."

"I know," she said, hating that even though he said it gently, it almost chastised her for believing otherwise. "I just meant… that it will be nice when we could do so with the luxury of no one questioning if we should be together all day."

He reached out, running his finger along her cheek in that way he did, almost as though she was a work of art that he was reviewing.

"I just want you to know what you are getting yourself into," he said. "I don't have the same life you are used to, and I do not want you to have any regrets."

"No regrets," she said firmly. "Not now, and not in the days to come."

She meant it. No one else had ever made her feel this way – cherished yet strong, not treated like she was the most fragile ornament on the tree.

Other women might not understand it, but then, they were not the ones who were going to marry Cooper Hartwell, now were they?

"Speaking of regrets," she said slowly, "does it bother you that we are marrying without your brother or any of your friends present?"

He was silent for a moment. "I am not sure that any of my friends are actually true friends," he said. "More acquaintances, as I haven't spent the time to get to know them. I'm also not even sure my brother would remember to attend the wedding. So, no, I am not concerned. All I care about is marrying you as soon as possible."

"Just tell me if that changes," she said. "Promise?"

"Of course," he replied. "But no regrets."

He leaned in, sealing his words with a kiss as he stared at her.

"Speaking of work, I have mine cut out for me," he said

with a grin. "I've done many jobs before, but never the work of a lady's maid. How do you think I'll do?"

"That depends," she said, trying not to smile back. "How much experience have you had in dressing women?"

He threw back his head and laughed. "Likely not nearly as much as you would guess. Come here, and I will show you what I can do."

She took his hand and allowed him to lift her. He cleaned her, dressed her, and while he certainly wasn't as fast nor as efficient as her lady's maid, he did everything reverently and with a great deal of care. When Noelle looked into the mirror, she was pleasantly surprised by how she looked – even if her hair was not quite as tightly pinned as it had been.

She was sure her maid would guess what had happened when she took the pins out later this evening, but so be it.

Noelle would soon be a wife, so she supposed this would soon be nothing out of the ordinary.

CHAPTER 23

*C*ooper welcomed the rest of the day with a very unfamiliar spring in his step, buoyed by his morning with Noelle. If this was a sign of things to come, he was a lucky, lucky man.

Even though there was a part of him that was still worried. They had only really come to know one another on what was – or was supposed to be – a holiday. What would happen when real life invaded, when she realized that time with him wasn't always fancy dinners and walks around a stately manor's gardens?

She was an intelligent woman, however. He had said it himself many times. She must not be naïve to the reality of what life would be like, although he was more aware than most that some situations needed to be lived before they could be truly understood.

"Hartwell, there you are."

Cooper turned with surprise to find Lord John was following him out of the breakfast room.

"You are looking for me?"

"I am. Could you spare a moment of your time?"

"I think I could fit in a meeting between the lighting of the yule log and Christmas carols," he said wryly, causing Lord John to chuckle.

"Good to hear. Meet me in the back parlor?"

Cooper nodded, following him toward the back of the house, wondering what Lord John might say. They found the back parlor empty, the room dark with expansive windows overlooking dead trees. At least Lady Burton had provided some festive décor, evergreen boughs winding around the top of the thick maroon velvet curtains, but she hadn't been quite as enthusiastic here as she had in the other areas of the house.

Cooper sat in the most comfortable chair in the room, which was still rather stiff. It was as though they had taken all unwanted furniture from throughout the manor and stuffed it all into this room.

"What can I do for you, Lord John?" he asked, placing his hands on his thighs as he waited to hear what the man had to say.

Yes, Cooper had gone to great lengths to be here to get to know gentlemen such as this one, but he was also aware that Lord John had closed off any favorable opinion toward him, and he wasn't about to grovel to gain his trust.

It wasn't worth it.

Lord John sat across from him, shifting back and forth in a chair that looked about ready to stand up and attack him.

"I must say, this has been the most interesting Christmas party I have ever attended, and Christmas hasn't even occurred yet."

"Agreed," Cooper said warily, wondering where this was going.

"I am man enough to admit when I am wrong, Hartwell, and I was wrong about you."

"Oh?" Cooper lifted an eyebrow.

"I was certain that you had murdered Northbridge. I was determined to avoid any connection with a murderer, which was part of the reason I was set against selling you any land."

"That only just occurred. You mean to say you weren't inclined to sell it to a man who wasn't of noble birth."

"That's part of it. But now that you are marrying Lady Noelle, you will be close enough."

Cooper leaned forward, studying him. "I thought my marriage to Lady Noelle was a strike against me."

"In a way, yes." Lord John said, tapping his fingers on his knee as his lips pursed together. "Look, if you're going to make me say it, I'll say it. Yours is the best offer. I thought another was coming to fruition, but now, with Northbridge gone, the deal has fallen apart."

Cooper snorted but accepted the truth.

"Is anyone attempting to resurrect it?" he asked, wondering just who his competition was.

"No," Lord John said. "Or I wouldn't be here."

"Look," Cooper said, moving forward again, his elbows on his knees. He had cultivated enough deals before to know that he couldn't show all of his cards or he would look too eager, and this could all fall through. "I'm a fair man. If selling your land isn't enough for you, I could make you a partner on this deal."

"Could you, now?"

"Why not?" Cooper shrugged. "I was in partnership before. I lost money there, but that is never a concern when I am at the helm. I've gotten myself this far from nothing."

If Lord John had a stake in this, he would be more inclined to lead Cooper to other opportunities and convince others to approve his schemes.

Lord John continued tapping, and Cooper could practically see his mind working as he considered his options.

Abruptly, Lord John stopped, stood, and held out his hand.

"Very well, Hartwell. You have a deal."

Cooper tamped down the joy that rose in him at coming closer to finalizing this deal. Instead, he calmly stood and took Lord John's hand.

"Very good. You will not be disappointed."

"I'd better not be," Lord John warned. "We'll settle all the contracts after Christmastide."

"Actually," Cooper said, placing his hands on his hips, "I'd like to get something in writing now."

"You don't trust me?"

"I'm a man of contracts," Cooper said. "I've relied on word in the past, and it hasn't served me well."

"So be it," Lord John said, although his tone held a trace of ire. "But my man-of-business will be difficult to contact at this time."

"Not to worry," Cooper said. "I am efficient at doing these things myself."

He had signed a contract with quite a lovely young woman not long ago – although she had been the one to create it. She had proven herself more adept than most of these men.

"You're sure all that changed was my innocence?" Cooper asked before Lord John could leave the room.

"That, and something Lord Andrew said to me."

"Which was?"

"The only good deal is the one made with a living man."

"I see," Cooper said as something tugged at the back of his mind, but he couldn't quite put a finger on it. "Thank you, Lord John. I look forward to doing business with you."

"And I with you," Lord John said. "Now, shall we go light this yule log?"

"I suppose we shall," Cooper said with a laugh as he

followed him out of the room and toward the front drawing room, where he could already hear the notes of "Hark! The Herald Angels Sing" playing. He turned the corner into the room, finding all the guests gathered, the room cold and the fireplace sitting empty, the log yet to be carried in and lit. It seemed the departure of Lady Jennifer, Lord Northbridge's body, and the coroner had left space for some of the Christmas spirit to return.

"There you are!" Lady Burton said. "The last of the guests have arrived. We can now begin."

Cooper met Noelle's eyes and saw the welcoming warmth within them when they rested on him. His steps were already taking him toward her, and he clasped his large hand around her much smaller one before he thought to hell with it and wrapped an arm around her shoulders, pulling her close to his side as he placed a chaste kiss on her temple.

"Is all well?" she said, tilting her head toward him.

"All is well," he confirmed, nuzzling her hair, her sweet cinnamon scent wafting around him.

"Thank you all for participating in this tradition that has so much meaning in our family," Lord Burton began. "Typically, the yule log is lit on Christmas Eve, but we like to do a little extra."

Laughter sounded throughout the room, for doing extra was often the case at Burton Manor.

"We have taken the tree we selected—thank you to my daughter, Hermione, and her companions for finding it—and have separated it into four sections so we will light a new log every evening until Christmas. We also have the ashes from last year's final section of yule log to light this one. Now, Smith!"

At his command, the door to the drawing room opened, revealing the butler, followed by two footmen carrying a large log. They placed it in the empty fireplace before exiting the room the way they came.

"Now for the lighting," Lord Burton said, igniting the kindling from a candle placed on the table. "This year's toast might be a bit different than usual, what with the strange Christmastide we have had so far," he said. "That being said, as much as we mourn Lord Northbridge and the circumstances of his death, may this be a reminder to enjoy each Christmas as it comes and celebrate the opportunity to spend this time with our close family and friends."

He moved the light to the yule log, and as the dry wood caught fire, the guests cheered and raised their glasses.

"Happy Christmas!" Lord Burton called out, and the rest of the guests responded in kind.

Cooper only had eyes for Noelle. Three days and it was going to be a happy Christmas indeed.

* * *

Cooper still smiled when he pushed open the door to his bedchamber that evening – a smile that turned quizzical when he heard a thump as the door hit something behind it.

"What in the world?" he murmured, peering around the door and slipping inside. The fire roared merrily in the fireplace, but he ignored it, too preoccupied with what awaited him.

It appeared to be a gift. He knelt and lifted the box. The lid was closed, while a large, shiny red ribbon was wrapped around it and tied on top in a perfect bow.

Was it from Noelle?

His heart thumped in anticipation of what she could have given him, even though Christmas was still a few days away. His mind raced as he thought of all the possibilities, deciding that his favorite idea was lovely undergarments that he could dress her in and then peel off her.

For there was no better gift to unwrap than Noelle herself.

He untied the bow slowly, savoring his surprise.

However, when he lifted the lid, it was with a frown as the contents were so far removed from what he had pictured.

The item appeared to be a children's toy – a wooden train, he realized as he slowly lifted it out. It was very crudely carved and was broken from what he could see. Who would give him something like this? He was turning it over in his hand when he heard a sound from behind him, and he jumped, his concentration wrecked.

His valet stood at the door, linen folded over his arm.

"My apologies, sir, for my lateness."

"You are not late—I am early tonight," Cooper said, returning the train to the box and placing the lid overtop.

He was still becoming used to having such a close, personal servant. His valet typically prepared clothing and organized his schedule, while Cooper chose to dress himself. He had known that arriving at an aristocrat's house without a servant would have only served to prove further that he did not belong there.

And so, Rogers had come with him.

"Rogers," he said abruptly, "do you know where this box came from?"

Rogers walked over and peered down at it. "No, I haven't seen it before. Nor was it here when I prepared your room earlier this evening."

"Very well. Thank you," Cooper said as Rogers filled his washbasin and set out his nightclothes before backing out of the room with a goodnight.

Cooper looked back at the box, shrugging. He had no idea what it meant or what to do with it, but he had other work to do now – prepare a contract for Lord John. He rubbed his hands together before walking over to his makeshift desk and pulling out a piece of parchment and quill pen.

Could this all come together as he planned? It was hard to believe, and yet, here it was.

It seemed almost too good to be true, which worried him.

For that usually proved to be the case.

CHAPTER 24

*T*he days were both rushing forward and crawling by at the slowest pace possible.

Now that their wedding was planned, Noelle just wanted the day to come – and yet, she had enjoyed this time to come to know Cooper better. She knew that once they returned to life in London, her time with him would be more limited, so she was taking full advantage of what she had now.

After all were abed that evening, she knocked softly on his bedroom door, but when no response came, she opened the door slowly to ensure he was alone before stepping inside. "Cooper?"

He was in a chair in the corner, bent over the bedside table he had moved in front of him like a desk.

He was so focused that he hadn't even heard her enter.

She walked softly toward him, wondering how to best announce her presence without scaring him.

"Cooper?" she said again gently, but he still jumped.

"Noelle!" he exclaimed, looking up and swiftly coming to her side. He wrapped his arms around her, providing her with the comfort that he had come to symbolize—comfort and desire that swirled up within her at his touch.

"I'm sorry. I knocked, but you must not have heard me."

"I was writing up a contract," he said, removing his glasses and rubbing the bridge of his nose. "Lord John agreed to sell me his land today – and become a partner on my deal."

Setting his glasses aside, he lifted her up in his arms, swinging her around in a circle, her feet an inch off the floor. She laughed in surprise and delight.

"Are you serious?"

"I am," he said, disbelief written on his face as he ran his hands over her cheeks. "It seems not being a murderer played to my favor. That, and his other deals falling through. I'm the only option left."

"How fortuitous," she said before pausing as some of the facts began to fall into place. "Not to lower the mood, but that leads me to something I have been thinking about." She furrowed her brow in concentration and bit her bottom lip.

"I love it when you think."

She laughed. "Well, you must love me most times of the day."

"I—" he stopped, his eyes wide as he stared at her, and she realized what she had said. Was it possible? Could he actually love her after this short period of time, after all that had occurred so far? He opened his mouth to speak again, but suddenly, she realized she couldn't bear it if he changed his mind and said something else, so she rushed to fill the silence instead.

"Anyway. I wanted to see you and hoped that—" her eyes caught on a box, sitting on the bed, perfectly wrapped in red ribbon. "What is that?"

He followed her gaze before dropping his arms and walking toward it, lifting off the lid.

"That is what I'm trying to determine," he said. "I found it behind the door when I entered my room tonight. It appears to be a broken train."

She furrowed her brow. What could that possibly mean? "Maybe it was meant for someone else," she said. "Can I see it?"

"Of course," he said, passing it over to her as she turned it over in her hands, her heart beating faster when she realized what this could be.

"Someone purposefully cut two of the wheels off this," she said. "Look at how it's perfectly sliced, as though a knife was used."

"I see that." He frowned, but instead of paying attention to the train, his gaze wandered back to the box. "Perhaps there is a clue as to who this is from," he murmured, turning the box over in his hands until a piece of paper fluttered out toward the floor. They exchanged a glance before he bent to pick it up

"Read it aloud, please," Noelle asked, even though she was already peering over his shoulder. He reached over for his glasses, fitting them over his nose.

Not all trains reach their destination. Best change course before this one derails.

That was it. No signature. No other words.

"Oh, Cooper," Noelle said, lifting a hand to cover her mouth. "That is definitely a threat."

He pressed his lips together. "It most certainly is," he said. "Someone doesn't want this railroad deal to go through. But who would care that much?"

Noelle rubbed her forehead. She had been thinking over this all day, and now, with this most recent threat to Cooper, it was all beginning to make more sense. "I think when we are considering who killed Lord Northbridge and who is threatening you now, we have overcomplicated everything. Trying to determine who is in a relationship with whom, where people were and when – we are missing the simplest part of it all."

"Which is?"

"If this railroad is built through Lord John's land, connecting London to Plymouth, who stands to lose the most? First, Sanderson disappears, as does the original deal. Then you heard of a new deal, one Lord Northbridge was organizing, and he is murdered. Now, you are trying to put forward a deal yourself, and you are threatened. If it wouldn't have been too suspicious to have another murder, then I would imagine you would not have been so lucky to have just been warned. Who would this hurt the most?"

"You're right," he said, crossing his arms over his chest. "We are making this far too complicated. But who would stand to lose from a railroad? It will only bring more people to the area."

"The stagecoach?" she said with a laugh.

"Somehow, I do not think the Royal Mail is out to get me."

"What about whoever owns the tollbooth to that area?"

"They will lose, that is certain, but is it enough to kill for?"

"I cannot see that being the case," she said. "But that does make me wonder... would the train cause travelers to miss a certain area? An area that makes a considerably great deal off the stagecoach passengers stopping through?"

"Surely someone must understand that the rail is coming, one way or another. If the one deal doesn't occur, another will be prepared within the next few weeks or months."

"Would there be a reason that a delay would help?" she asked, and he pursed his lips together before shaking his head.

"That, I do not know."

"Well, let's plot your route and see where would be underserved by this venture."

"Lucky for us, I already have a map."

He walked over to his bags, pulling out all of the documentation for the railroad, saved from the initial deal he had been part of and the one he had been working on since he had arrived. He unrolled a large map and spread it over the bed, weighing down the corners so they could better see it. He traced a line over the proposed route, from London down to the final stop.

"There are stops along the way, of course, but a traveler would not need to spend the night or dine in anymore," he murmured. "And Devizes is missed completely."

"It's not like an entire village is after stopping this deal."

"No," he mused. "But what about the land owner around said village? How much could he have to lose?"

"I suppose it depends on what he owns," she said, meeting his eye, hope rising that they might figure this out.

"I'll send a letter and get my men on this," he said. "I would ask Lord Burton if he had any information, but I'm not certain who to trust at this point."

"Hopefully, we will know soon," she said. "And no longer be living with a killer."

"That's the goal," he said with a chuckle. "We will only have to worry about one another. As much as I have enjoyed this Christmas party, I am already looking forward to leaving here – with you."

"You're not one to idle the days by, are you?"

"Most certainly not."

"Well," she said, sliding her hands up his chest until they wrapped around his neck, one hand plucking his glasses off his face. "In the meantime, I can think of ways to pass the time."

He chuckled again. "Did I tell you that I like the way you think?"

"The time for thinking is over," she said. "Time to show you."

And she most certainly did.

* * *

THE FOLLOWING two days passed in a blur of greenery, mistletoe, and wedding planning. Noelle had tried to urge Lady Burton not to make the wedding a great event, but Lady Burton was not to be deterred.

She had hosted many a Christmas party before, but never a Christmas wedding – and she would do this one right, in grand style, especially after the party's beginnings.

Noelle could only sigh and allow her to do as she pleased, for the truth was, none of it mattered – not as long as she had Cooper. He had wedged himself into her life in a way she had never expected. And now she was going to be his wife.

Their nights had been full of passion, which she had greatly enjoyed. However, she was becoming frustrated because she wanted *all* of Cooper—all of his love and all of his body. He insisted, however, that they wait until their wedding night to truly join together.

Hattie broke through her thoughts as she and Hermione sat on the soft chairs in Noelle's bedroom while she went through her wardrobe to decide which dress was most appropriate for her wedding.

She hadn't exactly planned for this.

"You will look beautiful in whatever you wear, Noelle," Hattie said wistfully as she held up a royal blue gown before shaking her head and returning it to the wardrobe. "The two of you make such a handsome couple."

"Thank you, Hattie," she said softly before turning to her friend and sitting beside her on the bed. "Are you sure this is all right? I know that the timing of the wedding is not ideal, not after what happened, and I understand if you would prefer—"

Hattie lifted a hand to stop her.

"What happened to Lord Northbridge was awful, and yes, of course, I am looking forward to someday planning my own wedding," she said. "However, that does not mean that you should postpone yours. Focusing on your wedding has helped all of us heal and still find joy in this Christmas season. For that, I am grateful."

"Thank you, Hattie," she said with a soft smile. "You are a good friend."

"As are you," Hattie said, her eyes watering. "I think you have saved my mother by saving her holiday party. This means so much to her."

"I'm glad," Noelle said, swallowing down the lump in her throat. "I am happy you are all here. Especially as my mother cannot be."

"You must miss her," Hermione said in a low voice, and Noelle nodded.

"Of course, I wish she could be here for my wedding. I never imagined the day without her."

"You know she is with you in spirit," Hattie said, squeezing her hand. "She would be proud of you, Noelle. And she would have loved Cooper and his charm."

"That she would have."

They all sniffed and dabbed handkerchiefs to their eyes before Hermione spoke up.

"I know this is rather forward," she began, breaking through the emotion in the room as Noelle and Hattie laughed, for Hermione was never anything *but* forward. Hermione rolled her eyes at them before continuing. "Do you love him?"

Noelle didn't even have to think about it. "I do."

"Does he love you?"

Had Hermione been reading her mind? Noelle paused, uncertain of how she should respond. She didn't want to lie, nor did she want anyone to think she and Cooper had any other reason to marry. She also wondered if their wedding could be the time he would realize or voice aloud his love for her. Or was he the type of man who would never truly fall in love? Was she reading too much into his actions, and was it more lust on his end? She wanted to believe he felt something deep and true for her. But could she be setting herself up for heartbreak?

"Cooper is not a man who easily shares his feelings," she finally settled on responding. "I have no problem sharing my thoughts with you, but I should keep his private."

"Very well," Hermione said, even though she had obviously seen through Noelle's words and understood that Noelle's feelings might not be reciprocated.

Noelle stood, returning to the wardrobe. Even though she had been staring at it all morning, it was as though someone had reached in and cleared all the other dresses away so that she could see what she was meant to. Perhaps her mother still had a hand in her life after all.

For there in the middle was the perfect dress—one she had packed herself, yes, but that she had forgotten about. It was cream with hints of red and gold embroidered around the hem and sleeves.

Perfect for a Christmas wedding.

"This one," she said, reaching in and pulling it up, holding it in front of her.

"It is beautiful," said Hattie wistfully, standing beside her.

"It's not white," Hermione noted, tilting her head to study her. "Most wedding gowns are white now."

Queen Victoria's white dress had made that customary, true, but it was not as though Noelle had any time to hire a seamstress to make her one.

"It is close enough, is it not?" she asked, sharing a glance with them. "It was my mother's."

"Then you absolutely must wear it," Hattie said emphatically. "You could also weave some holly into your hair, and you would be the most beautiful Christmas bride there ever was."

"Tomorrow morning," Noelle whispered, unable to believe it herself.

"Tomorrow," Hattie said with a smile, squeezing her arms. "It will be perfect."

CHAPTER 25

*C*hristmas Eve morning dawned as the perfect
winter day.

Overnight, snow had blanketed the grounds from beyond
the windows, while the trees were wearing a layer of hoar-
frost that was breathtaking.

Noelle would have been married outdoors beneath one of
them if she had the choice.

But with their license, the vicar married them in Guilford, a short carriage ride away, but at least they would have
the opportunity to walk below the beauty before and after
the ceremony as they traveled from the house to the awaiting
carriages.

She and Cooper had decided not to see one another last
night to avoid any bad luck, which they certainly didn't need
at the moment.

Now, Noelle stood at the back of the church on her
father's arm as the guests awaited them on the few pews at
the front.

She hid behind the wall by the door so that Cooper

wouldn't see her as her father stared at her, blinking away his tears.

"Noelle," he said, patting her hand where it rested on his arm, "you look magnificent."

"Thank you, Father," she said, as her heart squeezed. Her father had his faults, that was certain, but she loved him as much as he loved her in turn. She knew that he had done his best.

"I hope you are not doing this for me," he said gruffly. "I know I have failed you as a father, and if this is not what you want, there is still time for us to walk away."

"Father, it would cause such scandal!"

"I know, but scandal is better than spending your life unhappy."

She turned to face him, meeting his eyes, which were so like hers, while her mother had gifted the rest of her features.

"I appreciate that, Father, I do," she said, considering that, but two months ago, this entire agreement had been concocted because of his actions, and if her father had spoken up sooner, she might have agreed. But now everything had changed. "However, I want to marry Cooper more than I want anything else. I am looking forward to being his wife. I love him."

Her father let out a sigh as his shoulders dropped in relief.

"I am glad to hear it. I have been worried that you were doing something you had no wish to do, even though Hartwell has promised me that he will take care of you, be true to you, and do what I couldn't."

"Which is what?"

"Look after you."

"You did a fine job, Father," she said with a watery smile. "Do not believe that you failed me. You provided me with so much love, which is what truly matters."

"You look just like her, you know," he said, voicing what

they were both thinking – that her mother should be here. "Absolutely beautiful."

"Thank you," she whispered, struggling to get the words out. "I wish she was here too, but I am so glad you are."

"Of course," he said, patting her hand again before clearing his throat. "Well, should we go get you married?"

"Most definitely," she said as he stepped forward, leading her down. Hattie began to play Beethoven on the piano, and Noelle lifted her head to meet Cooper's gaze as they stepped into the very short aisle.

The moment he saw her, Cooper's jaw dropped and his eyes softened, filling with a look of vulnerability she knew that he never shared with anyone else. He opened and closed his mouth a couple of times as though he wanted to say something, and when Noelle and her father met him at the front, he shocked her by wiping away moisture from the side of his eyes.

"Are you all right?" she whispered, and he nodded.

"More than all right," he said, shaking her father's hand and then returning his attention to her. "You are stunning."

"Thank you," she said, looking him up and down, so dapper in his dark gray tailcoat and trousers. "You are not so bad yourself."

They laughed with one another, forgetting the rest of the room until the vicar cleared his throat and lifted his book in front of him.

Noelle had been so focused on Cooper that she hadn't looked around the church itself. While she was accustomed to simple decoration in a church, Lady Burton had sent servants ahead to prepare for the wedding and, of course, had outdone herself. Greenery hung from hooks and rails to cascade around them, lit candles set within the boughs. Noelle wondered if any evergreens were left in the forest beyond. Noelle had to laugh when she looked up and saw the mistletoe hanging so obviously right above them.

She met Cooper's eyes, seeing the humor there as the chaplain read his opening blessing and introduction.

She didn't pay much attention to his words until it came time for them to exchange their vows. As she promised to "love, cherish, and obey," she infused all of the love she had yet to tell Cooper about into the words. She could have sworn she felt it returned when he promised to "love, honor, and keep" her in return.

The words were written into the book of prayer, yes, and she felt, in her heart, that they shared love now, love that tied them together in a greater bond than a contract ever could.

"It is now time to give the ring," the chaplain said, and Cooper held her trembling hand in his as he reached his other hand into his pocket to pull out the gold band. Noelle gasped when she saw the setting.

It was beautiful, yes, but it was not just any ring.

It was her mother's.

She looked up from the ring to meet Cooper's gaze, seeing him watching her with some hesitation.

"Is this all right?" he whispered, to which she could only nod as she tried to prevent the tears from spilling out and falling over her face.

"More than all right," she said. "It's perfect."

He slid the ring, inlaid with small but beautiful rubies and diamonds, onto her finger. It fit perfectly, as she had known it would.

The prayers and blessings that followed were a blur, until it was time to sign the marriage register.

As Noelle sat at the small table that had been placed beside the altar, she picked up her pen to sign, unable to stop herself from peering over her shoulder up at Cooper.

"Another contract," she said with a grin.

"One that can never be broken," he said with an answering smile, kissing the top of her head, right above the holly berries woven through her curls, as per Hattie's recommendation.

She signed it before passing him the pen and showing him where to sign. He leaned over before placing another kiss on her temple, his lips resting just beside her ear.

"You are all I ever need," he said.

He then leaned over and signed the page flourishingly, solidifying their everlasting marriage contract. One that would be unbreakable.

She had never been happier.

* * *

COOPER HAD BROKERED MANY DEALS.

Raised himself in life from having nothing to being able to make possible anything he desired.

He had repeatedly proven himself and achieved everything he could ever have dreamed about.

And he could never remember being as happy as he was now, married to Noelle.

He stared at her from across the room, watching her as she laughed with her friends. He loved that she kept glancing over her shoulder, catching his eye, reminding him that even if they weren't standing right next to one another, they still shared a bond that was impossible to break.

His wife.

He shook the hands of the gentlemen who came over to congratulate him, but he had difficulty focusing on any of the conversations as he was too fixated on Noelle. They had already finished the wedding breakfast, but as the guests had nowhere else to be, they remained in the drawing room with one another.

"Hartwell, congratulations," Lord John said, extending his hand, "on both the wedding and the contract. We are officially partners."

"Glad to hear it," Cooper said with a grin. He prided himself on creating a straightforward contract, and he was glad the deal had been ratified.

"What's this now?" Lord Andrew asked, joining them. "The two of you are in business together?"

Cooper straightened, glancing over at Lord John, who appeared just as uncomfortable as he felt. He would have preferred that they not discuss this with anyone else, especially after he and Noelle suspected the murderer's motive might be due to this railway deal, but he hadn't shared the need for secrecy with Lord John.

"We are going to do a deal together, yes," Cooper said with a tight smile, hoping Lord Andrew would drop it, but he was to be disappointed.

"Is this regarding the railroad?" Lord Andrew said, lowering his voice and stepping closer. Cooper could see the brother's gaze upon them, and he also started over. Cooper had a feeling that whatever Lord Andrew knew Lord Rochester would as well, whether he was present or not.

"It is," he confirmed. It would be public knowledge soon enough, so he could hardly lie, although he would have preferred the news didn't spread until they were no longer in the same house as a killer.

"Are you going ahead with it, then?" Lord Andrew asked, his brows drawing together in surprise. "Even after what happened to Sanderson and Northbridge?"

"I hadn't realized that Northbridge was still involved in a deal," Cooper said, feigning ignorance, even as he felt rather than saw Noelle drawing toward him, twirling a piece of mistletoe in her hands.

"Ah…" The other gentlemen shared a look of uncertainty before Lord Rochester answered.

"He was until his death. Dead men can't do deals."

"There have been some discussions. Nothing solidified as of yet," said Lord John.

"Well, it is still a fine idea," Cooper said. "One that you are more than welcome to take part in. Perhaps after Christmas, we can discuss it further. But you must excuse me, gentlemen, for my wife is approaching and deserves my full attention today."

They all murmured their understanding as he stepped away toward Noelle.

He had never seen a woman more beautiful. Of course, she was perfection when she was garbed in absolutely nothing, but her attire today was breathtaking.

"You are so beautiful," he murmured as he looked her over again, holding her away from him. "If you must wear clothing, this dress is the best I have ever seen."

"Thank you," she said, stepping back with a smile. Her gown lacked the grandeur that many dresses of the day held. Instead, it was long, flowing from the bodice with simple cap sleeves. "It is not in style, but it was my mother's and therefore holds great meaning."

"I am so glad you could wear it," he said.

"Did my father give you her ring?"

"He did," Cooper said, reaching out and wiping the stray tear from the corner of her eye, even though he knew that she would never have let it fall in such a public setting. "He said it had always been for you, even when your mother was still with you. A way to connect the two of you, no matter where you are."

"I'm so grateful," she said, leaning her cheek into his palm. He loved that she didn't care what anyone else thought about them or what they were doing, that she showed her affection for him so naturally.

"Do you remember the morning you joined me in my bedroom?" she asked, looking up at him through her ridiculously long lashes.

"Love, I will remember that day for the rest of my life."

She smiled seductively. "We are married and while I highly anticipate our wedding night, I think a wedding day is in order – don't you?"

He swallowed at her suggestion. They had come so close to making love before, and he had imagined it more times than he could even admit to himself. Waiting the entire day now had seemed torturous.

"I would have a hard time disagreeing with that."

She reached down and took his hand.

"Let's go."

They managed to keep their pace to a walk as they exited the room, but the moment they were out of sight, they exchanged a glance, and as laughter bubbled out of Noelle, he answered with his own chuckle as they ran up the stairs as though they were being chased.

At this point, if they were caught, what did it matter? They were married, and the worst thing that could happen was that some guests would look down upon them.

Too late for that.

CHAPTER 26

*C*ooper told himself to take this slow and enjoy it. Enjoy Noelle, her body, her soul, and all that she had to offer him.

But he was having a hard time holding himself back. She was just too damn tempting.

He unbuttoned his jacket and slipped the sleeves off his arms before setting it on the chair beside him, remembering somewhere through his haze of desire that they would have to redress later.

But that wasn't anything to be concerned with at the moment.

As Noelle turned to shut the door behind them, he reached out, sliding his hands around her hips. She inhaled sharply as he moved with her across the room until they were sitting in front of the dresser, where he turned her around and pressed their bodies flush together.

"I know that it isn't Christmas quite yet," he murmured in her ear, "but I think we should start a new tradition along with our marriage."

"What is that?" she asked, her voice breathy.

"Unwrapping a gift a day early," he said.

"Oh?" she said, her voice raspy. "What kind of gift were you thinking of?"

"You," he said, tracing his thumbs over her hip bones. He could get used to this style of dress, which allowed him to feel her every curve when he slid his hands along the fabric.

A beautiful pink flush began to stain her skin, blossoming out of the dress and running up her neck until it flooded her cheeks.

He wanted to gather her in his arms and hold her close, while at the same time her sensuality was impossible to ignore. She was everything he had ever wanted but hadn't known would ever be within his reach.

And, unlike the reason why this all started, it had nothing to do with her social standing or who her father was. He would have married her all over again if she had lived in the same neighborhood where he was born.

He finally allowed his eyes to dip down to focus on the creamy expanse of her bosom that was pushed up over the bodice of the gown. It had been covered earlier with her mantle during the ceremony as they had walked outside, but the moment she had removed it during the wedding break-fast, he had nearly jumped across the table and carried her upstairs.

Thankfully, he had learned to show restraint, only now he couldn't help the way his cock was thickening in his trousers.

He stepped back, unbuttoning his shirt slowly, a smile tugging at his lips as he watched how she lifted her hand to the back of her neck when he began to show her some of his skin. Good. She should be as taunted as he was earlier.

Her eyes danced over him without any shame as he enjoyed exposing himself to her.

"You are a confident man, Cooper."

"It's easy when I've captured a woman like you."

He could tell how much she wanted him, although he didn't think anyone could desire anything more than he did her.

"Your turn," he said, reaching out and running his fingers along that tempting bosom, and she shrugged one arm through her sleeve before following with the other side. Her skin was pale against the fabric of her thin chemise below, allowing the outline of her nipples to peek through.

His heart raced in anticipation, which had truly been building since the moment he had laid eyes on her weeks ago at that charity ball.

"Need some help?" he asked, and she nodded, turning around to allow him to slip the fastenings through the holes at the back of her dress. When he reached the last one, the dress slid down to the floor, and he took a moment to bend down and lay it over the other chair.

By the time he returned, she had lost her chemise, and he was overcome once more by her incredible beauty. How perfect her breasts were, the pale pink nipples calling to him.

And now, she was his in truth. He didn't have to hold himself back. He reached out, gently stroking her breasts, his thumb gliding over her nipples, her breasts generous in his hands. Her curves were soft, supple, and made for his touch.

He dipped his head, wrapping his lips around one nipple, sucking it deeply into his mouth as her cinnamon scent invaded all of his senses. She threaded her fingers into his hair, her nails scraping over his scalp, causing him to tremble.

Finding her too low beneath him, he picked her up and deposited her on the surface of the dresser before him, moving his lips to her other breast.

"Cooper," she sighed as she stretched her legs out, circling his hips and pulling her toward him. She reached down, wrapping her hand beneath his jaw before lifting his face to hers. The moment their lips connected, she swirled her tongue into his mouth, the desire a heady taste that made him desperate for more.

He slid his hands up her bare legs, laughing when he found she still wore the boots she had donned for the wedding in the chapel. He unlaced them with one hand while continuing to kiss her, before throwing the boots behind him, allowing them to clatter to the floor.

Once those were discarded, he picked her up, his hands palming her bare bottom, soft and made for his hands. He laid her back on the bed as gently as he could, while she reached between them and began to stroke him through his trousers.

It nearly did him in right there, and he lifted himself up, his hands fisted on the mattress beside her head.

"One moment," he said as he undid the fastening and rid himself of them rather clumsily for a man who did so every day. She seemed to have taken away all the rational thought he usually held.

Her eyes were heavy on him as he threw them to the floor to join her boots, no longer caring about their state when they redressed later. Hell, he would prefer to stay in bed until the arrival of the new year, anyway.

She bit her lip and moved backward up the bed, spreading her legs for him. He had never seen anything so damn perfect.

The mattress dipped under his weight as he crawled toward her, wanting to pounce on her but knowing that he needed to take this slow. It was hard to remember that this was her first time, after all they had shared.

When he finally reached her, he held himself above her as he ran a hand down her body until he found her hot, ready center. She squirmed when he began to caress her gently but then pushed him farther down, encouraging his fingers harder, deeper. She rode his hand, and he nearly choked at his amazement. He had never met a woman who was so unabashedly herself, who didn't hold back from showing what she wanted and how she liked it.

He thrust in and out as she arched her chest toward him, and he dipped his head, giving her breasts the attention they deserved. His fingers and mouth moved in rhythm until he found he nearly couldn't take it anymore.

Apparently, she felt the same, for she pushed him up away from her as she wrapped her legs around him again.

"I need you now. Please, Cooper."

She didn't need to ask twice.

He removed his fingers and positioned his cock between her thighs. As he slowly pushed into her, she bit her lip, and while she felt fucking fantastic around him, he also knew that he shouldn't rush her, reminded himself that this was her first time.

She was slick, tight, and yet she stilled He couldn't lose control.

Not yet.

He breathed deeply as he waited for her, until her eyes met his. Despite the slight hesitancy held there, she nodded to him.

"You're all right?"

"Fine," she breathed. "Just fine."

He reached down, circling her sensitive bud again to try to remind her of how good this could feel, and soon enough, she was arching her hips off the bed, her breasts straining toward him.

He took that as a sign and began moving again, slowly at first, but as she rocked with him, her breath quickening, he soon found that he couldn't hold back any longer, and he thrust in hard, deep, fast, until she was crying out his name and clenching around him as she came.

It was all he needed to let go, and he pressed his face into her neck as he emptied inside of her, shaking with an unmatched intensity.

He stayed within her for moments, long enough to return to himself, until he finally rolled to the side. He had enough wherewithal to stand and find her linen, helping her clean up before moving back on the bed beside her, watching her as she came down from their exertions. Her cheeks were flushed, no longer just pink but a deep red.

"Noelle," he said, taking her cheeks in his hands. "Are you all right?"

"More than all right," she said, her brown eyes sparking delightfully. "That was all that I could have wished for and more. Yes, it hurt initially, but Cooper, I never knew such pleasure could be possible."

His grin was so wide it nearly split his cheeks.

"Well, we can do it again, as often as we like," he said before turning serious again. "Listen, I know the nobility likes their separate bedrooms and formalities, even between married couples, but I like how it is where I'm from. We spend every night together, sleeping or not."

"I think I can get behind that," she whispered as she stared into his eyes.

"Good," he said, "because I wasn't going to prepare you another bedroom when we get home."

Home. It felt so good to think that they would soon share one.

"Does this mean that you want to amend our contract?"

"Just which contract is that?" he said, raising a brow as a lock of hair fell over his forehead, and Noelle reached up to push it back. "We've signed a few now."

She laughed. "When we decided to marry in truth, you had said this would be a marriage in name. That I could go about my business, and you would not be concerned with coming home to me. Is that still our plan?"

His eyes searched hers. "Do you want it to be?"

"No," she said, boldly lifting her head to him, even as her heart beat quickly, waiting for his denial.

"Then it won't be," he said simply. "We will live as a husband and wife are expected to live."

That was still open to interpretation, but Noelle would take it for now. It was better than the original agreement.

"Are you any closer to determining who might be the murderer?" she asked, not wanting to think of it but also knowing that they couldn't truly move on while under threat.

"I have a few ideas," he said. "All I need to confirm my theory is to determine who owns the land we discussed. I should receive the letter at any moment. I do know, however, that it can't have been Lord Bingly. Someone set him up. Just like I think I would have been set up had you not provided me such unbreakable verification for my whereabouts."

"Which led to our marriage," she said, shaking her head, for she would never have guessed this would be the result of that impulsive declaration and yet was so grateful it had turned out this way.

"It was the best decision you ever made," he said with a laugh.

"Speaking of marriage," she said, "do you think anyone would notice if we just... oh, I don't know, didn't return to the party for the rest of the day?"

He sighed. "I wish I could say that it would be fine, but I have a feeling that they would miss us, especially since this is our wedding day."

"Oh yes," she said. "There is that. And Christmas tomorrow."

"We shall have to light the last of the yule logs, and I

assume there will be church and dinner," he said. "And then… well, real life will begin."

"I can hardly wait," she said with a smile, tugging him close and kissing him again.

"Truly?"

"Truly," she said, stroking his face as she smiled at him.

It was on the tip of his tongue to tell her what she meant to him, but he couldn't find the right words and wasn't sure if this was the right time. He had never been a man to say much about his emotions. It was hard to find time to say how one felt when the family was trying to survive the day.

But he would have to learn how soon enough because this woman was remarkable, and he needed her to know it.

The right time would come.

He would have to be patient.

CHAPTER 27

$\mathcal{T}$heir absence that afternoon had not gone unnoticed, but fortunately, they merely received a few ribbing remarks from the younger set and some stern glances from the older.

Noelle could handle both of them.

She'd married a man she loved – even if she hadn't told him yet.

It was Christmas. Life was perfect.

Yes, there was still the business of an unsolved murder, but she imagined they could get through anything as long as they had one another.

The Christmas Eve feast would be second only to Christmas dinner, and Noelle was famished after her rather... rigorous afternoon.

Hermione watched her eat with a raised eyebrow while Brighton made more than one snide comment. Noelle chalked it up to jealousy, and when the ladies retired after dinner, she found that she was so caught up in what was to come once more that evening that she hadn't been paying attention to the conversation.

When the men finally joined them, she nearly jumped off the sofa to find Cooper, but a glance around the men filing in told her what her heart already knew – he wasn't there.

He had told her that he was going to ask Lord John to review a couple of things about their deal that had been nagging at him, but she had hoped he would do so while the men were together.

Except… there was Lord John in the corner, talking to Hermione. So where could Cooper be?

Perhaps he had excused himself for a few minutes or was walking the grounds as he did when he became over-whelmed. She sighed out her impatience and decided that she wouldn't wait around. She was finished with this party for the evening and ready to start her wedding night – even though she'd already had a wedding afternoon. A newly married woman could take what she wanted.

She decided she would start looking for him at his library desk and perhaps in the orangery, which had become a secret place for them. He would often hide away there if he needed space from the party.

Well, there or the grounds, but the wind was howling fiercely tonight, and she had no desire to find her outdoor garments to see if he had left the house.

She would have to wait until he returned if he was out for a walk.

No one paid her attention as she left her seat, placing her drink on the table by the drawing room door before contin-uing through the foyer and then on to the back of the house.

The doors to the library were open, and when she walked through them, a gust of cold air reached her. Had the terrace doors been left open? She shivered as she stepped into the usually warm and cheery room.

"Cooper? Are you in here?" No response. "Is *anyone* in here?"

She heard nothing but the wind sweeping in through the doors, and she rushed across the room, looking outside to see if Cooper had perhaps left to walk in the snow. She couldn't see him leaving the doors open behind him, but perhaps they had blown open accidentally.

She was about to shut them when she saw a figure heading toward the house, cloak billowing behind him.

"Cooper!" she called out in relief as the darkened figure approached. "There you are. I was so worried."

The man looked up at her and stopped abruptly before marching toward her again, his steps more hurried. Noelle frowned. His gait was unfamiliar, and the closer he came, the more she realized his stature was wrong. This wasn't Cooper.

His face lifted toward the house, the sconces within the room shining just bright enough for her to make out his features in the dim light.

It was Lord Andrew or Lord Rochester. She couldn't be sure which from this distance.

And the sneer on his face was not one that she recognized. She paused for a moment. She had known these men since she was a child. They had been raised in the same circles, had attended the same events, and had even been mentioned in the same conversations regarding marriage at one point.

But this man... this was not a man she knew.

Realizing the threat, she backed away, shutting the doors as quickly as possible.

Panic dulled her senses as she searched for the lock as he reached the terrace. She knew that he would only push open the doors and catch her if she turned and ran. Her movements became frantic, but she cried out in relief when she finally found the mechanism and turned the lock just in time.

He reached the door, trying the knob, banging his fist

against the glass with a thud when it denied him, causing her to jump.

She backed away slowly, terrorized by the menacing look in his eyes – terrorized but livid. Angry that he would scare her like this, angry that he might have played a part in the murder of Lord Northbridge. Why else would he look at her like that, with such hatred in his eyes? She had known him since they were children, and he had no reason to hold any malice against her.

Unless… her heart started beating erratically when her mind cleared slightly now that the initial threat had vanished, realizing what this could mean.

Cooper was missing. Could this man have had something to do with it?

She hadn't stopped walking backward and suddenly bumped into a bookshelf just as she noted a strange look of recognition on the face of the man banging on the door. It was almost… relief?

And then, suddenly, the supposed bookshelf behind her moved.

Her breath caught in her throat as she turned around slowly, looking up into the face that matched the one outside the door.

This was Lord Rochester.

Meaning outside was Lord Andrew.

Only, there was no safety to be found here. For not only did these men wear identical faces, but their expressions currently matched.

Holding malice and, to her dawning horror, satisfaction.

For they had caught her.

Cooper groaned as he came to, the room in front of him swimming into focus.

The first thing he noticed was the cold. It was freezing here, his breath smoking in the air before him. A room of plain wooden boards surrounded him; the furniture dark shapes in the dim light. A tiny candle smelling of tallow burned on the table beside him, meaning he had little time until it would be extinguished altogether.

He tried to move his hands, but they were tied together with rope that scratched into his bound wrists.

He blinked rapidly, trying to focus on what had happened, how he had gotten here, and, most importantly – how he would escape this predicament.

There was also something nagging at him, something far more important.

Oh, yes. Why had they not just killed him outright?

He didn't have long to think about it, however, for the door burst open, allowing in a gust of cold winter air, snow, and Lord Rochester. Or was it Lord Andrew? Cooper couldn't be certain, for his focus was as fuzzy as the light.

It had taken both of them to subdue him and carry him here. Of that, he was sure.

"You're awake."

"What the fuck is happening?" he demanded, and Lord Andrew – yes, this was Lord Andrew – grinned at him.

"Oh, what fun we are going to have. In fact, the fun has already started."

The pieces of Cooper's memories began to join together. He had been walking out of the dining room with the other gentlemen, ready to rejoin the women. He and Lord John had planned to discuss their deal, but Lord John asked for a moment with one of the women first – Lady Hermione, if Cooper was not mistaken. He couldn't see what Lord John saw in the woman, but that was neither his business nor his problem.

As they exited the dining room, the butler had approached and held out a letter to him that hopefully contained the information he had asked from one of his men of business regarding the land he had wondered about.

Before he could open it, however, Lord Rochester had asked for a moment to speak to him, suggesting the library. Cooper had been wary, keeping the man in his sights. Then everything had gone black when they had walked through the doors. Cooper must have been hit on the head. There was no other explanation.

And Lord Andrew must have done it. The brothers were working together.

This begged the question – where was Lord Rochester right now?

And why was Cooper here and not lying on the ground, dead by gunshot like Lord Northbridge?

"Why the fuck am I still alive?" he demanded.

"Such language," Lord Andrew said, shaking his head at him. "And that accent. Your true self is coming out."

"I've never been anything but my true self," Cooper retorted. "Not like some people."

"We are doing what we must do to preserve our way of life," Lord Andrew said. He dragged a chair across the floor toward him, the sound grating on Cooper. "If only all of you fortune hunters would stay out of it."

"Is that what Lord Northbridge was? A fortune hunter? Thought he was your friend."

"He was more of an acquaintance," Lord Andrew said, crossing one leg over his other. "And in this case, he didn't understand that he needed to keep his nose out of where it didn't belong."

"Why not just warn him off of this deal?"

"He was ruining everything. He tried to keep you out of this, to send you home. Do you remember being locked in the orangery? It was his juvenile attempt to keep you from knowing what we were doing with our deal."

"But you stood up for me to him."

"Because we knew that we might need you to blame if things went wrong – which they did, of course. You would have been such an easy scapegoat if Noelle hadn't turned on all of us and backed you up. So we had to plant that pistol in Bingly's room – not that he was the most believable murderer."

He said it as though it was Cooper's fault that he hadn't been able to frame him.

"You didn't answer my question."

"Oh, why are you still alive? Well, to kill you outright would bring too much scrutiny upon us after Northbridge. We had to make this believable and not put the true motive in question."

"So, you have an alternative?"

"Why, yes, we do." His grin was sickeningly sweet. "You are a newlywed, but it will come to light that your new wife wasn't as pleased as she seemed with the marriage. She came to her senses and told you she no longer wanted to be with you and would return home with her father instead. In a fit of rage, you killed her, and then you killed yourself in grief. You will leave a note, of course."

Anger grew within Cooper at every word, so strong that he nearly used it to break the bonds that tied his wrists.

"You would never get away with something like that."

"Would I not? You see, Hartwell, not many people question a lord, which my brother is, if you haven't noticed. You? You are no one without your money. No one cares about you."

Someone did. His wife. Who he had to protect with every

part of him. He wished desperately that she was staying in the drawing room with the other ladies, that she would realize by his absence that something was amiss. He might not make it out of here, but he had to ensure she didn't go down with him. It was no fault of hers that he had wanted to be part of this deal.

Was it his own greed that had brought him here? Should he have just dropped this when everyone associated with this rail line had gone missing?

Most likely.

But it was too late for that now.

"Why do you care so much about this railway deal?" he asked, still needing to know, even though the circumstances had overcome him. "You must understand that it will happen one way or the other, at some time or another, whether you like it or not."

"That might be true," Lord Andrew said, "but we are going to be part of it and ensure that it takes the route we need it to and stops both when and where we want it to."

"Then why not just be a part of it from the start?"

"Because we need more time. Time to raise our own capital. Unlike what you might think, we're not all sitting around on stacks of coin like Northbridge was. My brother and I need to earn our way forward, which happens once a year – at a little festival near our estate called The St. Swithin's Summer Fayre."

The ire that had been simmering in Cooper's family threatened to explode at the extent these men had gone to – although he wasn't surprised. He had seen people do far worse for far less.

"So you needed one more summer season?"

"That's right. One more year, and we should have enough. But not if your damn railroad gets built through there first. We would not only lose out on the railroad but also on all of the people who would bypass the town. People learn about the festival while stopping through overnight when travelling."

"None of this is worth killing for."

"We didn't think so, either – not at first. But then when we took Sanderson just to scare him, we accidentally went too far, and you know what? It wasn't as difficult as we thought and made everything much easier for us."

Cooper cursed, inwardly this time. Here, he'd thought this party would open up opportunities for him. Instead, he had only embroiled himself in a murderous scheme and a love that had wrapped itself around his heart – which was likely more dangerous than anything else could ever be.

For if anything happened to Noelle, he would never forgive himself.

Nor be able to live without her.

"So, what now?"

"Now, you wait," Lord Andrew said far too cheerfully. "Your wife should have been here by now. I best see what's taking my brother so long. Fear not. You will be reunited momentarily."

That didn't give him a lot of time.

He had to get them out of this.

And he had to do it quickly.

CHAPTER 28

*N*oelle's feet were frozen in her boots by the time she was pushed through the door into the small cabin. It must have been the gamekeeper's cottage, which she was sure had long been abandoned based on the stale air surrounding her as she walked through the room, Lord Rochester pushing her forward.

But she wasn't alone.

"Cooper!" she cried when her eyes adjusted to the light.

He was sitting across the room, and the look in his eyes as he raised his head was murderous.

Not at her, of course. His gaze softened when it reached her, before returning to the two men who had followed her in. They hadn't even covered her with a cloak, and she was shaking so furiously that she wondered if she would ever be warm again.

If they found their way out of this, that was.

"We can stage this without her," Cooper said, his voice darker and more menacing than she had ever heard before. "Let her return."

"Even if that was possible," Lord Andrew said, "we cannot

allow her out of this. Not now, with all that she knows. It's too late."

"She's freezing," Cooper insisted. "Give her a cloak, at the very least."

"It won't matter much soon," Lord Rochester said, the brothers wearing twin smiles of death more sinister than anything he had ever seen before. "She doesn't have much time left in this winter."

Cooper let out a growl of rage that would have frightened Noelle if she hadn't known the soft, gentle side within him.

She found his gaze, hoping he could read the emotion in her expression and understand just how much she cared about him. If this was the end, he had to know how much she loved him. She wished she had told him when they still had the chance.

It was a wonder he wasn't angry enough to overcome the two men, which he likely would have were his hands not bound together behind his back.

A thought struck her, one borne out of desperation or her love for him, she wasn't sure, but it might be enough to create a chance.

"Before the end, can I give him one more kiss goodbye?" she asked, not having to fabricate the tremor in her voice.

The twins exchanged a glance.

"Go ahead," Lord Rochester said, waving his hand forward. "Make it quick."

On shaky legs, she made her way across the small room to Cooper until her face was inches from his.

"Cooper," she whispered, and all of the anger melted away.

"Noelle," he whispered back. "I'm so sorry."

"None of that," she said, cupping his face. "I have to tell you something."

He lifted his brows, speaking before she could. "You need to try to run."

"I will never do so without you," she vowed, "but I do have an idea."

She began to wrap her arms around him, hoping the brothers wouldn't see what she was doing in the dim light.

"Hurry it up," Lord Andrew said impatiently.

"Cooper," she said again, their noses touching. "I love you. So much."

His head nodded once, stiffly, as water rose in his eyes.

"I love you too. I should have told you. I should have—"

"None of that," she said, nearly grunting as she slipped the rope over his wrists. It had been tied tight, but from the evidence of blood on his wrists, she guessed that he had been working hard to loosen his bonds.

"It doesn't matter when we said it. We said it. We feel it. Now," she lowered her voice, "see if you can pull your hands apart."

He grunted, but she only heard the snap because she was so close.

"Stand up," came the command from behind them, and Noelle slowly rose, although she didn't step away from Cooper.

Lord Andrew was holding a gun out, trained upon both of them.

"How could you?" she lashed out, looking from one of the brothers to the other. "I thought we were friends! We have known each other our entire lives."

"Do any of us really know one another?" Lord Rochester asked with a smirk. "You knew who we wanted you to think we were. You did not know the men we truly are. What we want from life."

"You were putting on an act."

"No more than your husband does."

229

"That is different," she countered. "He does what he must to fit in where he needs to be, but he is still the same person on the inside, where it matters. I do not even recognize the two of you anymore. The practical jokers? The men who are quick to make everyone laugh? That is not who you are. Not anymore."

"We never were," Lord Andrew said. "And that is enough theatrics. Step away from him. We need to kill you first."

"You will not!" Cooper's voice of rage came from behind her, and at the touch of his hand on her hip, she stepped out of the way as he sprang forward, knocking Lord Andrew down. The gun went spiraling away just as the door burst open behind them. Unable to spare any time to see who it was, Noelle leaped forward for the gun, reaching it seconds before Lord Rochester. She wrapped her hands around it, trying to lift it, as Lord Rochester came barrelling toward her. She tried to pull the trigger, but it seemed to be stuck... or perhaps she just didn't have it in her to be a killer, no matter what he had done to her and Cooper.

Either way, she braced, ready for the attack, but then he flew to the side, knocked away, and she stopped, staring slack-jawed ahead of her.

"Lord John?" she squeaked out, her heart beating as she wondered whether he would be friend or foe.

She looked to the side, only to find Cooper standing above Lord Andrew, the man out cold on the floor beneath him, having succumbed to Cooper's rage, his nose bloody and his head angled to the side.

Ignoring Lord John momentarily, she rushed across the room, throwing herself into Cooper's arms, which wrapped around her instantly.

"You're safe. You're alive," she said as he buried his face in her hair, the two of them holding on as tightly as possible, never wanting to let go.

Cooper came back to the moment first, looking over her head at Lord John, who was watching them while basically sitting on top of a protesting Lord Rochester.

"How did you find us out here?" he asked.

"I went to find you where we were to meet. One of the library doors was open, and when I looked through them, I could see two figures dragging a woman away. With all that has occurred as of late, it certainly wasn't something to ignore, so I followed. I heard enough before I entered."

"You took awhile."

Lord John shrugged. "Perhaps it was a touch too late," he admitted. "But all has ended well, has it not?"

"We should be grateful Lord John is here," Noelle said, patting her hand on Cooper's chest, unable to stop the shaking that had overcome her, although whether it was due to the cold or the shock of everything that had just happened, she couldn't be sure. "No one would have otherwise believed us."

"You're right," Cooper said with a sigh.

"What do we do now?" she asked.

"Now, we return to the house and take care of you," Cooper said. "Then Lord John and I will clean up this mess."

"The magistrate is not going to be pleased about returning, especially on Christmas," Lord John said with a sigh, which caused a bubble of laughter to well up from within Noelle – misplaced laughter, she realized at the same time as Cooper seemed to. He hugged her tightly against his side.

"Let's get you back to the house."

"Take my cloak," Lord John said, and Noelle saw Cooper biting his cheek, likely trying to keep his thoughts to himself that Lord John had taken the time to fetch his cloak despite seeing Noelle being hauled off by two men into the cold night.

But he had come, hadn't he? So, they should be grateful.

They were alive and together.

That was all that mattered.

* * *

Cooper had spent many Decembers as a child without any Christmas spirit, but he had never had a Christmas like this before.

There wasn't much that could save this Christmas party now – not with one guest murdered and another two now rightfully and most publicly accused as the murderers.

At least the sorry sod that was Lord Bingly had finally emerged from his room, where he had been spending most of his days and nights since his accusations, too ashamed to face the party, even though he hadn't done anything wrong.

Cooper couldn't quite understand it. If it had been him who had been falsely accused, he would have done everything in his power to right the scenario. But then, that was what made each man different, was it not?

Thankfully, Lord John explained most of what happened once they had all gathered near the foyer of the house. It seemed that the disappearance of four guests had caused quite the stir, and they had all been searching for them for a time, concerned that something was amiss.

Something was, indeed, very amiss.

"What are we supposed to do?" Lord Burton asked, seemingly at a loss for once in his life. He looked around at all of them as though they had the answers, but this was not exactly a common occurrence.

"Right now, I have tied them to the chairs in the game-keeper's cottage where they held Mr. Hartwell and Lady Noelle – ah, Mrs. Hartwell, I should say," Lord John said. "Unlike when poor Bingly here was accused, I wouldn't suggest that we let them return to their rooms."

"All we can do is to call the magistrate tomorrow, I suppose," Lord Burton said with his largest sigh of the party. "Then return them to London and let them be dealt with there. I can send some of my men with them and hope that they are not led astray on the way there."

The remaining few men murmured their agreement and tense silence reigned until Hattie's sniffles cut through the air.

"I can hardly believe it," she said. "Poor Lord Northbridge."

"Since we've dispensed with all propriety, Lady Hattie," Lord John said as he tapped his cap against his leg, "I'll tell you that Lord Northbridge wasn't much of a catch. While I don't wish the man dead, you should be glad that you didn't marry him."

Lady Burton gasped at that, but Lord John only shrugged. "It's the truth. Just ask your other daughter."

Hermione gasped at that, but Lord John continued on, this incident apparently unleashing all of the truths within him.

"Another truth is that I think we will all hold a special bond after this. Whether it is one we welcome or not, I have no idea, but we will certainly never forget this Christmas, now, shall we?"

"Is it still your favorite time of the year?" Cooper murmured in Noelle's ear, and she nodded as she turned to him.

"Much has happened at or near Christmas that is not in my favor. My mother's death, and now this kidnapping and murder. But you know, a lot of good has happened too. I felt so much love at this time of year as a child, and now, it is our wedding anniversary. So, I do not suppose a time of year can hold that much malice. It is more what you *do* with that time, you know?"

He placed a kiss on her forehead as he held her close against him, breathing her in and grateful for all that she brought to him.

"Have I ever told you how smart you are?" he asked in a low voice.

"A few times," she laughed, but as she did so, she shivered, and he reminded himself that they couldn't take any more time down here, for they needed to get her comfortable again.

"Well, as much as we would like to stay and visit with you all, I need to be getting Noelle warmed up," Cooper said, and they all murmured their understanding. "Could a bath be prepared, please?"

"Of course," Lady Burton responded as she walked out of the room, likely in search of a maid. "Goodnight."

He wrapped his arm around Noelle as they exited the drawing room. Once they walked through the entrance, he slipped his other arm beneath her knees and lifted her.

"What are you doing?" she asked wondrously, and he squeezed her close.

"Carrying my bride, of course."

The truth was, he could feel her utter exhaustion, but he also didn't want to make her feel weak.

For she wasn't. She was the strongest woman he had ever met.

And he loved her fiercely.

He had wasted time not telling her sooner.

But he would spend the rest of his life making it up to her.

CHAPTER 29

$\mathcal{T}$he hot bath warmed her and returned some of her senses – although her toes coming back to life had been excruciating – but it didn't heal Noelle of the trauma she had been through.

However, Cooper sitting next to her and waiting had undoubtedly helped.

As she snuggled into him now, she closed her eyes in the comfort he provided – comfort and the knowledge that he wasn't going anywhere.

"That was quite the wedding day," he said as they lay face-to-face on the pillow, staring at one another. His eyes were all over her, as though he was trying to memorize her every feature.

"Certainly unforgettable," she quipped, although his features remained serious.

"I don't know what I would have done if anything had happened to you," he said. "I would never have forgiven myself."

"Then we are fortunate that it ended as it did," she said. "But I do not doubt that it did so because of you – and because of what you and I are to one another. I understood what you were thinking, what you wanted me to do. We are connected by more than our marriage vows, although that has certainly strengthened them."

"I believe that's called love," he said before clearing his throat. "I should have said it to you sooner. I felt it quite some time ago. I just... I have never had that love in my life before. My family didn't love as yours did, and it took me some time to accept it, for I know that my life will never be the same again."

"Do you regret it – falling in love?" she whispered, wondering if she genuinely wanted to know his answer.

"Not at all," he said, causing relief to rush through her. "Being in love is the greatest emotion that could ever overcome me. To such an extent that no matter what happens, it will always be worth it, and I would accept it again and again, as long as it was with you."

His words warmed her entire body more than the bath ever could have as she smiled at him.

"You are right in that I have known love my entire life, and yet I was still scared to tell you how I felt," she said, lowering her lashes. "I shouldn't have feared it, but if you hadn't accepted it – accepted *me* – I would have had difficulty in continuing the fake relationship. Then once we had committed ourselves to one another, I could never have walked away."

"Well, you're stuck with me now," he grinned.

"Thank goodness."

He kissed her on the forehead.

"Sleep now. We will talk more about tomorrow in the morning."

"It won't be tomorrow then."

"No. It will be Christmas. And our new life together will be born."

"I can hardly wait," she said, the smile playing on her lips as she drifted off to sleep.

* * *

COOPER SHOULD HAVE SLEPT MORE, but he couldn't keep his eyes off of Noelle – even in her sleep. He watched her in awe and protection – two emotions he never thought he would attach to a woman.

When her eyes blinked open the following day, he brushed the hair away from her face. She pushed herself up on one elbow, her lips curving into a smile.

"Good morning," she whispered. "Happy Christmas."

"Same to you," he said. "How does it feel waking up as Mrs. Hartwell?"

"I am grateful I can do so in your arms," she said. "It's hard to believe this will be every morning."

"Does that scare you?"

"Not at all. It leaves me feeling at peace." She smiled lazily at him. "I have something for you."

"Oh?"

She slid out of bed and over to the corner cabinet, where she had hidden away his gift. It was wrapped in brown paper, as she hadn't wanted to elaborately wrap it and remind him of the previous, much more threatening, package he had received.

"Here," she said, placing it his lap as he sat leaning against the wooden headboard. It looked small in his large fingers, but he quickly opened it, eagerness on his face as he did so. She wondered when he had last received a Christmas gift.

He held the creation in front of him, and Noelle's heart pounded in excitement at him receiving it as well as hope that he would like it.

"You made this," he said in wonder, and she nodded. "When would you have had time to make this for me?"

"Usually before bed," she said with a slight smile, "until you otherwise distracted me. What do you think?"

He slid the pair of gloves over his fingers, which fit perfectly. She had stitched his initials on the right hand glove and hers on the left.

"How did you know my size?" he asked, blinking at her.

"I've gotten to know your hands rather well," she said, heat stealing up her cheeks. He chuckled as he leaned forward and kissed her lips. "Your hands were always cold, and you never wore gloves. Maybe you preferred not to, but I thought you might need them."

"Thank you. I love them."

An hour later, Noelle finally made her way to her own chambers to prepare for the day. They would all attend a Christmas church service, traveling there on sleighs; apparently, snow had blanketed the ground overnight.

Cooper waited for Noelle to head downstairs for breakfast, uncertain of what they would find.

The dining room was rather tense and formal, as though no one was quite sure how to act around one another.

"Good morning," Noelle said as she sat next to Hattie, patting her hand as Cooper pushed her chair in. "Happy Christmas."

Everyone murmured their response as Lady Burton sat next to the head of the table, obviously blinking away her tears at her ruined Christmas party.

Cooper tried to choke down some ham, but the air was so stilted that it was difficult. The Christmas spirit, as Noelle had told him about time and again, was completely stifled.

It might not be his place, but he would not allow her first Christmas as his wife to be in such circumstances.

He stood, pushing his chair back with a scrape.

"Listen, I understand that these are not the most ideal of circumstances," he said as all the eyes around the table turned toward him in shock – including Noelle's. However, she didn't say anything. She sat back and watched him with interest. "But there are a few things that I have learned, both in my past and here over this party. First, our time here is never guaranteed – as we know from what happened to Lord Northbridge. The second is that we should take advantage of the moments we have to spend with those people who are important to us. I might have just met most of you, but you have all been in Noelle's life for a long time. Christmas is a time to celebrate, even if our circumstances are not ideal. We are no longer under any threat. So why do we not appreciate Lady Burton's considerable efforts to host such a lovely party and embrace this Christmas?"

Jaws dropped open. Lord John was laughing behind his hand. Lady Burton's tears were now falling down her face.

But heads were also nodding, as though they had all needed his speech to snap them out of this melancholy and remind them of what was important.

"That was lovely, Cooper, thank you," Noelle said, placing her hand on his arm as he retook his seat.

"Yes, well done, chap," Lord John said as he tilted his drink down toward him, and Lady Burton murmured a teary thank you.

It took a few minutes, but soon, conversation resumed to its normal levels, and Cooper breathed a sigh of relief.

There wasn't much time for pleasantries as they soon had to leave for church in nearby Guilford. The sleigh ride was cold but joyful, the wind whipping the hair of the ladies out of their careful pins and caps as they all snuggled deep underneath the blankets. Cooper certainly took advantage, holding Noelle close to him to share his warmth and enjoy her body. He didn't think he would ever tire of that.

The church was rustic, but comfortable. Only a small bit of greenery remained from the grandeur of their wedding the day before. The service was short and simple, reminding Cooper of the Christmas celebrations he attended as a child.

By the time they arrived back to Burton Manor and dinner was prepared, it seemed that most of the party had returned to how it had been planned – with the exceptions of the prisoners in the gamekeepers' cottage, of course, guarded by rotating footmen.

He accepted a generous glass of bourbon from one of the footmen as they waited for dinner in the drawing room, kissing Noelle on the forehead before she crossed the room to speak to her friends.

Lord John soon joined him with a drink of his own.

"What is it like, being a married man?" he asked as he took a healthy sip, saluting Cooper first.

"It is more than I ever could have imagined it to be," he said truthfully. "I never thought I wanted to be married, if I am being honest. And now I can't imagine my life without her."

"Interesting," Lord John murmured into his drink. "Not a sentiment I believe I will share."

"You never know," Cooper said with a laugh. "I suppose you and I will see more of one another now that we are in partnership."

"I suppose we shall," Lord John said, clearing his throat, his gaze on the drink he was swirling around in his hand. Finally, he looked up at Cooper with some chagrin in his eyes. "I would be remiss if I didn't apologize."

"For?"

"For my rudeness when you first arrived," he said. "I judged you for no reason other than your birth, and I was wrong. Which was certainly proven when men I grew up with turned out to be murderers."

"I appreciate that," Cooper said, surprised that he would admit to such wrongdoing. He held out his hand. "Let's leave all that in the past, shall we?"

"Agreed. Thank you," Lord John said as Lord Walters approached. "I'll leave you to your dinner, then."

"Mr. Hartwell," Lord Walters said with a nod. "Is this everything you ever thought it would be?"

"So much more than that," Cooper said as they chuckled. "And you should call me Cooper now that we are family."

"Of course," Lord Walters said. "Welcome to the family. You have been a surprise, I must admit."

"How so?"

"I thought you would be all business. I knew you would care for my daughter, but I assumed the support would be financial. I am glad that she has found love. She deserves it, and, it seems, so do you."

"Thank you," Cooper said. "I will make sure to take care of the whole family." He fixed him with a look. "And I am happy to advise on any investments going forward, should you require my help – or Noelle's."

Lord Walters chuckled ruefully. "As I am sure you have gathered, I am not proficient in that area."

"We all have our strengths," Cooper said. "And you love your daughter, which is the greatest strength of all."

They both stared over at Noelle as she laughed, appreciating the magnificent woman she was.

For love transcended all of life's stations – especially when a woman as special as she was involved.

* * *

NOELLE WAS PLEASED that her friends were still enjoying themselves despite the tribulations this house party had provided.

"Are you all right with everything, Lucy?" she asked, as Lord John's sister stood with her hands clasped in front of her, gazing dreamily about.

"What do you mean?" she asked, blinking back at them. Her head had always lived more in the clouds that in the present moment.

"You and Lord Andrew had a... connection, did you not?"

"Oh," she said, waving her hand in front of her. "We were just having a bit of fun. Nothing too serious." She shuddered. "It is hard to believe what he did, though."

"It will take some time to understand it all," Lady Brighton said, biting her lip, and they were silent for a moment, although Hattie didn't seem to be giving them any attention.

"Who do you keep looking at?" Noelle asked Hattie, following her gaze. "Lord Bingly?"

Hattie's cheeks turned an immediate dark shade of pink. "I've always found him rather adorable, but it wasn't until this house party that I realized I cared more about him than I thought. When he was accused of murder, I could hardly believe it, and I realized afterward that I was... disappointed."

"Why do you not go speak to him?" Noelle said.

"I had rather hoped he would approach me first."

Hermione rolled her eyes while Noelle gently prodded, "I'm not sure that Lord Bingly is the type to make the first gesture. Besides, after everything that has happened, he is probably even shyer than usual."

"You can do it, Hattie," Lady Brighton said, placing a hand on the small of her back as she pushed her forward, and they watched her go.

Lord Bingly's face color matched hers, but they were both happy and blushing as they chatted.

"Well, that just might end well after everything," Hermione said, and Noelle nodded. "Promise that no matter how busy you become as a wife, you will still find time for us?"

"Of course!" Noelle said, grasping her hand. "Always."

Lady Burton walked over and asked Hermione to play a song on the piano, and she sighed at the idea before doing as she was told. Seeing her father speaking to Cooper, Noelle wandered over to them, smiling at the two men who meant the most to her.

"This was quite the Christmas party, wasn't it?" she said before placing her hand on her father's arm. "Are you going to be well?"

"I am," he said before clearing his throat. "Actually... I have something I wanted to speak to you about."

Noelle waited.

"I am going to ask Lady Crupley to marry me."

Noelle knew her mouth must have dropped open in shock, and she exchanged a glance with Cooper, who looked just as surprised.

"That is... wonderful, Father. I didn't know you were interested in Lady Crupley – nor in marrying again."

"We have been talking to one another in our time here, and while we might not share the love that your mother and I did, she is a good woman, and we are both on our own. We might as well support one another. I suppose you inspired me, Noelle."

"That is lovely, Father, truly," she said before stepping forward and embracing him. "Anything you need, please let me know."

"Of course."

They watched him walk away, over to Lady Crupley, before looking at one another and bursting into laughter.

"I did not expect that at all," Noelle said.

"Do you mind?"

"Not at all," she said. "I was concerned about him being alone. I am glad to hear that he will have someone."

"I agree," Cooper said before looking toward the window. "With this continuing snowfall, we might have to leave in the morning, even though the party is not yet finished. Is that all right?"

"It is," Noelle nodded. "I am ready to begin life with you, away from this party. Take me home?"

"With pleasure," he said, taking her in his arms and kissing her soundly. "Isn't it something? We thought that, at this point, we would be finding a time to dissolve our contrived betrothal. And instead—"

"We are leaving married," she finished with a laugh. "I wouldn't have it any other way."

"I suppose I gifted myself a bride for Christmas," he grinned. "A gift that I will never top."

"You could say that our marriage will be a gift that keeps giving."

"You are right about many things," he said. "But that, I think, is the most accurate of all. Now, come, let us prepare to leave on the morrow."

"Where a new Christmas will begin."

"Christmas – and the rest of our lives."

EPILOGUE

ONE YEAR LATER

"*H*ow are you feeling about this decision?" Cooper asked as he held out a hand to Noelle and she took her first step up the staircase.

"Perfect," she said with a smile, looking up at the most dapper man she had ever seen in her entire life. "I wouldn't want to be anywhere – or with anyone – else."

"Even if you miss a triumphant return to a Christmas party?"

"Especially so," she said with a laugh as she walked up the last few steps to join Cooper on the train. Cooper's brother, Trenton, followed them up the stairs but left them at the top to find his own train car and likely additional entertainment.

It was the first journey the train would make on the new route that Cooper had backed. The line wasn't complete— there was still plenty of track to lay—but it would reach the first stop, which was quite the feat when they had only finalized their deals less than a year ago.

With only one week until Christmas, the other partners hadn't been certain about the timing for this maiden voyage, but Cooper had insisted that it was perfect.

Noelle knew he would be right—he always was, as he had such instincts about these matters.

It had been the best year of her life with Cooper, even with the odd bit of uncertainty, including the trials of Lord Rochester and Lord Andrew in the House of Lords. They had both been held guilty of murder and, while they would have been hanged were they anyone else, they had been transported to Australia instead.

Most of the money they had stolen from Sanderson and the original investors had also been found and returned— and then reinvested into this very railway they were riding on today.

Cooper led her to the rail to look over the London station, wrapping his arm around her back as they stared out.

"Soon, we will have been married a year," he said, nuzzling her nose.

"I hope you have chosen a magnificent anniversary gift for me," she said, looking back at him over her shoulder. "One that is differentiated from my Christmas gift."

He threw back his head and laughed. "That is one decision that will haunt me for the rest of my life, I think?"

"Most decidedly so."

"Well, it is worth it," he said before removing his arm for a moment. He was dangling a small box over her shoulder when he returned it.

"For you."

"But—"

"I know Christmas is still a week away, but I wanted to give this to you now. The timing couldn't be better."

She eyed him suspiciously before lifting the small lid of the box, her eyes widening at its contents.

"It's a key," she said.

"It is," he confirmed. "Your powers of observation are quite adept."

She poked him in the side.

"Just what does this key unlock?"

"My heart?"

"Cooper!"

"Very well. It unlocks a manor house."

"A manor house. Whose?"

"Yours. Ours. Well, if you agree to it."

Her brows furrowed together as she affixed that stern expression on her face. "Could you please just tell me what's going on?"

"I'm trying to!" he said, holding his hands up in front of him in surrender as he laughed. "There is a manor house for sale in Somerset, where we will stop in a few hours. If you liked it, I thought we could purchase it to have a little place in the country. They have agreed to sell it to me as long as you like what you see."

"A house? Cooper, you didn't need to do that!"

While she knew he could afford it, it seemed like too much. Over the past year, she had appreciated how hard he worked but how he still made sure that she knew she was his priority and had found the balance between spending time with her and doing what was necessary for his work.

"I know," he said before looking away from her as he became quiet. "But I have seen the yearning in your eyes sometimes when we are looking out the window. I know you enjoy London, but you also miss your time in the country."

"That is a very spoiled way for me to think," she said, although she didn't argue his point.

"Well, lucky for you, I am much richer than most of the lords you could have married."

"That is not why I married you, and you know it." She swatted him.

"I know. You married me for my other assets," he said, wiggling his brows suggestively as she rolled her eyes.

"Well, if you love it, I will love it," she said, turning around so they were face-to-face and chest-to-chest. "I love everything you do for me. You could not be more considerate of me, and I appreciate you so much for that."

"I also can't keep my hands off of you," he said, causing her to laugh.

"Please don't stop that," she said. "But truly. I love you. And you do not have to gift me a house yearly for Christmas."

His face suddenly went slack. "I made a big mistake, didn't I? I shall never be able to top this gift."

"No," she said with an exaggerated sigh. "You most certainly will not. But you have given me so much. Our London home is beautiful, and you have given me full leave to do as I wish. Now this?"

"Well," he said with a small smile. "It was partly selfish. We can travel here in mere hours on our train line. But I think it is also a good place to raise children, is it not?"

They both looked down at her stomach, which had yet to show the signs but was already holding new life.

"It will," she smiled back at him just before the train gave a lurch and started moving forward. Nearly simultaneously, the first speck of snow fell from the sky, landing on Noelle's nose. Even though it melted, Cooper leaned forward and wiped it off.

"You know, some would say what we have is too good to be true," he said, staring down at her.

"I would have thought that myself in the past," she said,

her lips curling. "But sometimes you just know when something is right. When we are where we are supposed to be, with whom we are supposed to be with."

"I agree. I love you, Noelle," he said, kissing her nose where the snowflake had landed. "Happy Christmas."

"And I love you," she said. "Happy Christmas, indeed."

* * *

Dear reader,

I hope you enjoyed Noelle and Cooper's Christmas story!

If you are in the midst of the Christmas season (or searching out the Christmas spirit at any time of the year), then I hope it finds you enjoying all of your traditions and the people you love.

In the upcoming pages, I will leave you with the first chapter of one of my first and favourite Christmas stories, Christmastide with His Countess. It is a story of an arranged marriage and second chances. I hope you enjoy.

If you haven't yet signed up for my newsletter, I would love to have you join! You will receive a free book as well as links to giveaways, sales, new releases, and stories about my coffee addiction, my struggle to keep my plants alive, and how much trouble one loveable wolf-lookalike dog can get into.

www.elliestclair.com/ellies-newsletter

Or you can join my Facebook group, Ellie St. Clair's Ever Afters, and stay in touch daily.

With love and Christmas spirit,
Ellie

* * *

Christmastide with his Countess

SCARLETT TANNON, Countess of Oxford, has not seen her husband since their wedding four months ago — which is exactly what she wanted. Schooled by her mother's experiences, Scarlett carefully guards her heart from any man, most especially her handsome and charming husband. She vows she will never suffer the heartbreak of her mother. Instead, she shares her love and gifts with those less fortunate than herself, including the tenants of her husband's lands — tenants he has ignored for too long.

Hunter Tannon, the Earl of Oxford, is devoted to his role in the House of Lords, determined to make a difference for those who are affected by his work there. Rejected by his bride, he leaves her on his country estate and puts her from his mind as he focuses on what really matters: political decisions. Until one day, his steward sends him an urgent summons to return his home in the country, a summons that Hunter cannot ignore or refuse.

No sooner has he returned, at the beginning of the Christmastide season, than Hunter finds himself stayed by a snowstorm. He is surprised when he sees his wife's frosty exterior beginning to melt, revealing a mysterious and sensual woman underneath. Will days together, in the presence of sleigh rides, mistletoe, and the Christmas spirit, drive them apart forever, or reveal to them a love they never thought possible?

AN EXCERPT FROM CHRISTMASTIDE WITH HIS COUNTESS

AUGUST, 1813

"*W*ilt thou have this man to be thy wedded husband, to live together after God's ordinance in the holy estate of Matrimony? Wilt thou obey him, and serve him, love, honor, and keep him in sickness and in health; and, forsaking all other, keep thee only unto him, so long as ye both shall live?"

An eerie silence came over the church as Scarlett stood there, breathing shallowly, heart pounding hard in her chest. She longed to toss her bouquet of herbs and pansies over the altar and turn on the heel of her soft pink kid slipper and run down the aisle — alone — just as fast as she possibly could.

She heard a cough behind her, a few muttered words, some whispers.

Out of the corner of her eye, she studied the stranger who stood at her elbow, now shifting back and forth from one foot to the other.

He was tall, much taller than her own average height. He was attractive, to be sure, the structure of his face chiseled as though it had been sculpted by a master. His dark, nearly black locks circled his head in a symphony of curls. She wasn't sure what color his eyes were, for she had yet to actually look at them.

The first time they had met was moments ago, when her father had deposited her here, at the front of the quaint village church.

She ran all of her options through her mind once more and eventually came to the only possible conclusion, the one that had led her here this morning.

"I will."

When she finally said the words, they rang out with strength and clarity, for Scarlett never said anything she didn't truly mean. She would marry him. She had no choice, despite the stirrings deep inside her soul that cried out for freedom. But freedom, it seemed, was proving elusive — for the moment, at least.

After confirming it was her father giving her hand away — of course, for she was moving from being considered one man's property to another's — the minister continued, placing her right hand in her betrothed's.

Her skin tingled where they touched, despite the thin material of her glove between them. As he repeated the words given to him by the minister, Scarlett finally looked up at him. She hadn't meant to, but it was as though she had no choice. She locked eyes with him, and once she did, she wished she hadn't.

For his eyes were of a blue-green unlike any color she had ever seen before, except perhaps in a body of water on a dark day. And it seemed they almost … twinkled? She blinked, trying to break the spell they had seemingly cast over her, but it was as though she was losing herself in their depths, drowning despite her best efforts to break through to the surface.

His voice was a silky smooth baritone, though she hardly heard a word that he said.

Suddenly there was silence again, and his lips turned up as he looked down at her. Was he nearly laughing? She stared back at him incredulously — what on earth was funny about this? Until she realized it was her turn to speak. Again.

"Can you repeat that?" she whispered to the minister, and he looked perturbed but did as she asked.

"I, Scarlett, take thee...." Oh, blast. What was his name again? Had the minister told her? She looked from him to her betrothed once more, and now his lips really did stretch out into a grin.

"Hunter," he supplied in a murmur, leaning into her, flustering her even more.

"Yes, I know, Hunter," she said. *Get a hold of yourself, Scarlett. You don't even want this wedding.* "I, Scarlett, take thee, Hunter, to be my wedded husband, to have and to hold from this day forward, for better for worse, for richer for poorer, in sickness and in health, to love, cherish, and to obey, till death us do part, according to God's holy ordinance; and thereto I give thee my troth."

The blessings and prayers went by quickly, and suddenly, nearly before she even realized it, the wedding was over, and her new husband — *husband* — was walking her down the aisle and out of the church.

Good Lord. What had she done?

* * *

HUNTER EYED the woman standing beside him. She was an attractive woman, that was to be sure. Her hair was a deep chestnut with a touch of color that reminded him of cinnamon flowing through it. A smattering of freckles dusted her flawless skin, which was somewhat darker than the porcelain of other young women with whom he was familiar. It was as though she spent time outdoors. Not that he would know. He knew nothing about her. He had barely known her name until today, for goodness sake, and she had certainly forgotten his.

Their marriage had been an arrangement between their parents. His father was a powerful marquess, hers an earl. There had been a planned meeting between the two of them, of course, but her parents had told him she was ill. As he spent nearly all of his time in London and she had always been in the country, another suitable time never arose. Finally, the wedding day was planned, arrived, and here they were.

He hadn't even been sure she would be in attendance at the ceremony, despite her father's assurances. When she had walked down the aisle toward him, her face was set in a grimace so fierce that he had nearly hidden behind the minister. Did she really abhor him so, a man she had never met?

And yet when she stood beside him, he could sense something else. She was angry, true, but perhaps almost — afraid?

She did not say a word to him through the wedding breakfast, nor to anyone else for that matter. She simply sat, as stoic as a soldier about to be sent into battle, as though she were waiting for the entire event to be over and done with.

Not that he blamed her for that, at the very least. This entire affair was so forced, there was nothing at all natural about it, and that very tension pervaded the room.

Eventually, all of the guests blessedly left, and he was standing alone with her at the cusp of the entryway of his — their — country estate.

"Scarlett," he began, turning toward her, but she remained resolutely stiff, looking out after the dirt kicked up by the carriages as they trundled away down his drive. "I gather this is not quite what you had imagined. I—"

"How did you gather that, oh, wise husband?"

He raised an eyebrow at her sarcasm. "By the petulant way in which you have conducted yourself since the moment you walked into the church."

"Excuse me?" Finally, he had her attention. She turned and looked at him with those eyes that had befuddled him so when they caught his during that moment in which he said his vows. They were hazel, as light as the cinnamon pieces running through her hair but with flecks of gold that danced when she had watched him closely as he had spoken the words to her that bound them together for the rest of their lives.

"I said—"

"I heard what you said. Is that any way to speak to your new wife?"

He crossed his arms over his chest. Who did she think she was, to snipe barbs at him so when he had done nothing but do as was expected of him, the same way she had?

"You have hardly uttered a word since you arrived in the village. You certainly have not spoken to *me*. You avoided me until the moment our wedding actually began. And now you are doing your best to push me away. Am I really so repulsive, Scarlett?"

She was silent for a moment, breaking their locked gaze as she stared out over the glorious gardens sweeping away from the front door, around the drive and out behind the house.

"I do not wish to be married," she said, her words stilted and angry. "Not to you, nor to anyone else."

"Then why did you agree to marry me?"

"I had no other choice. My father deemed this wedding to be, and so be it. It was that or try to make my own way in the world, and as much as I would like to, I simply … could not. And you? Why agree to marry me, a woman you have never met?"

"I had business to see to, as I always do. I did not have time to meet and properly court a woman. My father was anxious for heirs. He assured me that you were a well-bred woman who would fit well within my life. He may be a cold man, but he has always seen to my best interests and I trusted him in this."

"You trusted your father to find the appropriate women with whom to spend the rest of your life?" She looked at him incredulously, and he shifted from one foot to the other. When she put it like that, it did sound rather idiotic, but at the time it had made sense. His father had told him she was beautiful, from a good family, and with a significant dowry. That had all been true. What he had never mentioned was her temperament.

Hunter was surprised when she was the first to break the ensuing silence.

"You have a beautiful home, at the very least."

"Thank you," he said, resolving to try to be civil with her. He had no wish to spend a life in conflict with his wife. He had enough of that in his day-to-day affairs, which he spent within the House of Lords. "I primarily live in London, but I have always loved Wintervale. It seemed the ideal place to hold the wedding celebrations. The village is lovely at this time of year, and I have known the minister since I was a child."

"You don't spend much time here?"

"Not really," he said with a shrug. "It seems I have too much requiring my attention in London."

"I see," she said, a contemplative look coming over her face, and he wished he could read her thoughts.

"I thought perhaps we could spend a month or so here before returning to London?" he asked. "I know it will be well in advance of the Season but—"

"Go," she said with a wave of her hand.

"Go?" he asked, confusion filling him. "We will travel together when the time comes."

She looked at him now, her hands on her hips. "I will be honest with you, Lord Oxford. I have no wish to go to London. Not in a month, not for the Season. I think I like it here, and here I will stay."

"But—" He desperately rifled through his mind for the right words to say. It would be rather untoward to show up to London without his wife for the entire Season. He must convince her to come, even for a short time. He took a breath. He was sure she would change her mind. She just needed time. "We will discuss it," he finally said, and she quirked up one side of her lips — the first resemblance to a smile he had seen since he'd met her.

"Very well," she said. "Now I wish to remove this monstrosity of a gown. If you will excuse me."

And with that, she turned, calling for her lady's maid. He followed her from a distance, studying her as she walked through Oak Hall, looking one way and then the other until she discovered the staircase at the end of the connecting Stone Hall. She lifted her "monstrosity," which was, in fact, a beautiful pink gown, though a bit frothy for his taste, up from the floor and started up the grand staircase. He followed her with his eyes all the way up, around the balustrade, and down the balcony that hung over the great room beneath, where he stood, wondering what in the hell had just happened.

He didn't see her again. Not through the afternoon, not

even for dinner, despite persistent knocks on her door. "I don't feel well," she had called out. And when he tried her door that evening, to determine how she felt and whether she had any interest in a marriage night, it was as he thought.

The door was locked.

* * *

KEEP READING Christmastide with His Countess!

ALSO BY ELLIE ST. CLAIR

The Scholar's Key

The Lord's Compass

The Heir's Fortune

The Remingtons of the Regency

The Mystery of the Debonair Duke

The Secret of the Dashing Detective

The Clue of the Brilliant Bastard

The Quest of the Reclusive Rogue

The Remingtons of the Regency Box Set

The Unconventional Ladies

Lady of Mystery

Lady of Fortune

Lady of Providence

Lady of Charade

The Unconventional Ladies Box Set

To the Time of the Highlanders

A Time to Wed

A Time to Love

A Time to Dream

Thieves of Desire

The Art of Stealing a Duke's Heart

A Jewel for the Taking

A Prize Worth Fighting For

Gambling for the Lost Lord's Love

Romance of a Robbery

Thieves of Desire Box Set

The Bluestocking Scandals

Designs on a Duke

Inventing the Viscount

Discovering the Baron

The Valet Experiment

Writing the Rake

Risking the Detective

A Noble Excavation

A Gentleman of Mystery

The Bluestocking Scandals Box Set: Books 1-4

The Bluestocking Scandals Box Set: Books 5-8

Blooming Brides

A Duke for Daisy

A Marquess for Marigold

An Earl for Iris

A Viscount for Violet

The Blooming Brides Box Set: Books 1-4

Happily Ever After

The Duke She Wished For

Someday Her Duke Will Come

Once Upon a Duke's Dream

He's a Duke, But I Love Him

Loved by the Viscount

Because the Earl Loved Me

Happily Ever After Box Set Books 1-3

Happily Ever After Box Set Books 4-6

The Victorian Highlanders

Duncan's Christmas - (prequel)

Callum's Vow

Finlay's Duty

Adam's Call

Roderick's Purpose

Peggy's Love

The Victorian Highlanders Box Set Books 1-5

Searching Hearts

Duke of Christmas (prequel)

Quest of Honor

Clue of Affection

Hearts of Trust

Hope of Romance

Promise of Redemption

Searching Hearts Box Set (Books 1-5)

For a full list of all of Ellie's books, please see
www.elliestclair.com/books.

ABOUT THE AUTHOR

 Ellie St. Clair is the creative mind behind Regency romances featuring strong, unconventional heroines and men who can't help but fall in love with them. Her novels perfectly blend passion, mystery, and suspense, transporting readers to a world where love conquers all, even the darkest secrets.

When she's not weaving tales of love and intrigue, Ellie can be found spending quality time with her husband, their children, and their beloved dog, Bear, a spirited husky cross. Despite her busy life, she still finds joy in the simple pleasures—whether it's savoring a scoop of her favorite ice cream, tending to her garden, or challenging herself in the gym. An avid plant enthusiast, she's on a never-ending quest to keep her indoor greenery thriving.

She also loves corresponding with readers, so be sure to contact her!

www.elliestclair.com
ellie@elliestclair.com

facebook.com/elliestclairauthor

x.com/ellie_stclair

instagram.com/elliestclairauthor

amazon.com/author/elliestclair

goodreads.com/elliestclair

bookbub.com/authors/elliest.clair

pinterest.com/elliestclair

Made in the USA
Coppell, TX
29 December 2024

43697443R00156